Ashdown Summer

ASHDOWN SUMMER

Colin Gaines

The Book Guild Ltd.
Sussex, England

The Book Guild Ltd
25 High Street,
Lewes, Sussex

First published 1990
© Colin Gaines 1990

Set in Baskerville
Typeset by Cable Graphics Ltd Eastbourne Sussex
Printed in Great Britain by
Antony Rowe Ltd
Chippenham, Wilts

British Library Cataloguing in Publication Data
Gaines, Colin 1922-
Ashdown Summer.
I. Title
823'.914 [F]
ISBN 0 86332 516 5

CONTENTS

INTRODUCTION

An old man wandering down the leafy lanes of Langentopf clutching the hand of his little grandson had become a regular sight in this rural corner of North-West Germany.

When young Rolf Muller was not at school, he would hang around impatiently for Grandpa to finish his breakfast so that they could be off on their morning walk. The lad was just nine years old when Grandfather Karl Muller had come to live with the family, and right from the start the little fellow had taken the old man under his wing. Unlike her big brother, Helga, aged three, was not interested in what their Grandfather had to offer, and after the first walk with them had opted for the company of her dolls.

Old Karl had a fund of wonderful tales to tell, and he found in his grandson a devoted listener. All the stories he told were from real life, his own, and he particularly fired the youngster's imagination with what he had to tell of his childhood days.

'When I was a small boy, my parents used to take me to England to stay with a distant relation, a very good friend of my father. Cousin Alex was a count and was also created a prince by Kaiser Wilhelm. His title was Alexander, Prince and Count Munster von Derneburg. He had a great mansion in a very large estate, Maresfield Park in the county of Sussex.'

The old man never once repeated himself, and yet he never ran out of stories. Prince Munster's two boys, Frederick and Paul, had been young Karl's constant companions on those holidays, being taken on outings by their governess Kitty, and Prewett the head coachman. One memorable Christmas they had been taken for a whole day in London. They had visited the Tower of London, and watched the changing of the guard outside Buckingham Palace. After lunch they had gone to a theatre to see a pantomine. Grandpa recalled that there had been a large cat that danced and talked, though he had no idea of what it said. There were funny men with painted faces and dressed in strange clothing who made all the children laugh and cheer. They had returned home late in the evening, tired but happy beyond words, and had made no protest when they were bundled off to bed.

Often in the summer they were taken to the seaside at Eastbourne where they would bathe in the sea, build sandcastles and occasionally would be taken out in a boat, with strong men pulling at the oars, to see the giant lighthouse at Beachy Head.

'To please Kitty and Prewett, we would go with them onto the promenade to listen to the band. Sometimes, when they thought we were not looking, we would see them holding hands. We thought this was great fun and we couldn't help giggling. It was very exciting for us when we were told that they were going to be married.'

Another of the stories was about a large expanse of woodland and common called Ashdown Forest. Thousands of trees of all kinds grew there, but there was also much open country where Kitty and Prewett used to take them for picnics. Looking for birds' nests, climbing trees, flying kites made for them by Prewett, games of hide and seek were made to sound like great adventure stories.

'Prewett told us many exciting tales about the forest; of highwaymen, bands of robbers, of smugglers coming up from the coast to discharge their loads of contraband. His accounts of the fights between the customs men and the smugglers were at times quite bloodcurdling. He showed us places which he said had been encampments of the early Crusaders on their way to the coast to take ship to The Holy Land.'

However much the old gentleman related, there was always more for another day. As the boy grew older, his affection for his grandfather never diminished, and even when he followed in the steps of his father and went on to Heidelberg, his letters home always held a separate message for Grandfather. Karl Muller had been a proud man when he had seen his son receive his graduation in medicine at Heidelberg, and he had experienced the same joy when his grandson had qualified for the same career in medicine.

When Karl Muller was seventy-eight years old, and Rolf a young man of twenty-five, the old man, feeling that he had but a short time to live, called for his grandson to come to him. Rolf was alarmed when he saw how feeble his grandfather had become, and he choked back a sob as he took hold of his hand.

'Grandfather, I had no idea how ill you were...'

'Never mind that, Rolf, there is something I must say to you. Listen to me very carefully. Do you remember the things I used to talk about when you were just a little boy?'

The old man began to cough, and Rolf passed him a drink of water.

'Do you think you ought to talk, Grandfather?' Rolf asked anxiously.

'Yes, yes my boy!' the old man returned impatiently. 'There isn't much time, and this is important. What I am about to tell you has never been told to a living soul, not even to your father.'

There was a gurgling sound coming from the back of old Karl's throat and Rolf, beginning to get alarmed, begged him to rest, but to no avail.

'No,' he spluttered impatiently, 'I'm all right; just listen. When I was last in England, it was the summer of 1914; war had just been declared between Germany and England, and my father's Cousin Alex was ordered to return to Germany immediately. Father was left behind to tie up the loose ends on the estate. I remember there was much activity, with servants and tradespeople dashing to and fro. No one had any time for me, a small boy. Consequently I was left very much to my own devices.'

'I clearly remember the village blacksmith arriving with a stout wooden chest on which were two large padlocks. Later that evening I watched my father, under cover of darkness, leading four workmen who were carrying a wooden chest. At times they appeared to be walking in circles but eventually, when they came to a part of the estate which I had never seen before, they came to a halt in a clearing. All I can remember about the place is that nearby there were five young oak trees in a row.'

'My father removed the blindfold of one of the men and ordered him to dig. After ten minutes his blindfold was replaced and he was told to rest. The other three men were each in turn given a similar amount of digging to do, and when a sufficiently large hole had been dug, the chest was lowered into it, and then Father himself filled in the hole. The four men, once again with their eyes covered, were led to a distant part of the estate where their blindfolds were removed. I watched in wonder at a discreet distance as my father took from his pocket what I took to be a small Bible. He opened it, and each man in turn was instructed to put his hand on the open pages and repeat certain words. After this was done, Father handed each a large bulging envelope.'

Having said all this, the old man told Rolf to look inside the top drawer of a cupboard and take out a folder. He handed it to his grandfather, who took from it a small pocket diary, its pages brown with age. The diary was for the year 1914.

'I want you to turn to the pages for the first week in August,' the old man said. There were several entries, but one in particular stood out from all the rest; it read simply:

MARESFIELD PARK - FIVE OAKS - THREE PACES
RIGHT.

Rolf returned the diary to its folder and replaced it in the cupboard. There was a faraway look in the old gentleman's eyes as he whispered hoarsely,

'Rolf, promise me that you will go and...'

The sentence was never finished. The old man went into a coma and never regained consciousness.

1

If you had a large enough map of East Sussex, and a particularly keen eye, you might make out the village of Maresfield, slightly to the north of Uckfield. To a stranger passing through it, there was little to attract attention, unless it was the pretty little church standing at the crossroads, and over on the other side the imposing Georgian hostelry known as *The Chequers Inn*.

The landlord of *The Chequers*, Charles Broxon, a thickset, ruddy-complexioned man of forty-five, stood at the end of the lounge bar talking to one of his customers, Chris Charnford, while Nancy the barmaid, assisted by her brother Percy, poured out drinks for the throng of thirsty men and women who had broken their journey to the coast on this Sunday in the middle of August.

Chris was the son of a local farmer, Arthur Charnford, who as well as farming kept a livery stable half a mile out of the village. Chris himself was something of a local hero in the field of point-to-point racing and in his late twenties, a bachelor whose interest in fillies was strictly limited to the four-legged variety. He would have been quite a catch for any one of the local maidens who often cast an admiring glance in his direction, but he was not for catching. His thick, dark curly hair wouldn't have looked out of place on a girl, but there was nothing effeminate about Chris. Six feet tall and broad shouldered, he was a match for any man.

Over in a corner of the room, three men were earnestly discussing the previous day's disastrous cricket match with Nutley village, a match which they had needed to win, but which had resulted in a crushing defeat. Most of the other occupants of the bar were, to use the landlord's description, passing trade or chance customers on their way south, the younger ones amongst them probably making for Brighton, and the more mature either to Bexhill or Eastbourne.

One man stood apart from the rest. He had no wish to be conspicuous, but being tall and athletic, with fair hair and very blue eyes, he attracted a lot of attention. From the manner in which he asked for his drink, he was clearly not English, although there was hardly a trace of accent in his cultured voice. 'A large beer please,' not, as an Englishman would have said,'a pint'.

When time was called the bar was quickly emptied, the regulars going home to a belated Sunday lunch, and others to their cars parked out at the back of the inn, ready to continue their journey. The young foreigner stayed behind, and walking over to where the landlord had begun checking the till, he enquired, 'Can you please tell me if you have any accommodation available?'

The landlord replied at once, without even lifting his head, 'Sorry sir. Just at the moment I can't help you; we have no room.' As he was saying this, his wife came up to them and, turning to her husband, she said,

'What was the young man saying, Charles. Did he say he requires a room?'

'Yes, but I've already told him we have nothing.'

'Oh, but we have, dear. Mrs Pearson checked out an hour ago, and Alice is changing the bed linen now.'

Turning to the young man, she gave him a welcoming smile and said, 'If you'll come this way, I'll show you the room.'

Charles Broxon was not pleased that his wife had gone to such pains to contradict him in front of a stranger, and he turned his back on them. This was something she had become accustomed to and she knew the resentment wouldn't last. She led the way up two short flights of stairs into a room which had already been prepared for re-occupation.

It was in no way like a typical hotel bedroom, where everything would have been of a standard pattern and predictable. It was the sort of room which immediatley made you feel at home, spacious, yet cosy. There had been no attempt at matching anything and to an interior designer it would have been an abomination, but to the young man who was to occupy it, it was perfect.

'We charge ten pounds a day for bed and breakfast,' she said, 'or sixty pounds for the week.'

'Thank you; I'm happy to take it. I should like to stay for two weeks, or perhaps a little longer.' Stretching out his hand towards her he said, 'I am Rolf Muller.'

Mrs Broxon took the hand, shook it gently, and reluctantly released it.

'Are you from Germany?' she asked.

'Yes! Do you mind?'

'It will be a pleasure having you,' she assured him.

Accompanying her down to the small reception alcove, he completed the registration formalities, insisting that he should pay in advance for his first week's accommodation. The lady assured him that this was quite unnecessary but nevertheless yielded to his firm persuasion.

Going out to the car park, Rolf opened the boot compartment of his pale blue Mercedes and took out two soft leather suitcases and a hold-all. He took them up to his room, declining the landlord's offer of assistance, and settled himself in. The room at the front of the building offered an excellent view of the church over to the left, and on the right was the lodge marking the entrance to Maresfield Park.

Unpacking as much of his luggage as he felt was necessary and arranging it in the wardrobe and drawers, he lay down on the comfortable bed. His long journey from Germany was beginning to tell on him and closing his eyes, he was soon asleep, oblivious of the noise of traffic passing under his window. How long he slept he neither knew nor cared, but when he awoke he felt refreshed and ready to take his first stroll on English soil.

With rising excitement, Rolf made his way through the archway supporting the upper floor of the lodge, the gateway to Maresfield Park, eager to set foot on the ground so often trodden by his dear old grandfather. Old Karl's description of The Park had been so vivid that his mind's eye had retained a vision of what it would be like. But what an anticlimax awaited him as he passed under the archway. The sight which now confronted him was nothing like the one he had imagined.

He found himself walking along a narrow roadway marked 'Private; Residents only', and on either side of this roadway were houses, some plainly visible from the road, but most of the larger ones discreetly hidden by tall hedges. Bemused, he walked on in the hope that he would eventually come across the mansion house where Prince Munster had once lived; but it was nowhere to be seen. There were few people about, and he covered almost half a mile before meeting someone to whom he might explain his dilemma.

The Reverend Percival and Mrs Truscott were returning home from their afternoon walk through The Park. With a brief 'good afternoon' they were ready to continue on their way, but the young man halted them by saying. 'Excuse me, can you please tell me what has been happening in The Park?'

They were taken aback and could think of no answer to the strange question.

'I am looking for the mansion house,' explained Rolf. 'Perhaps I have come to the wrong place.'

Seeing the look of utter dismay on the young man's face, Mrs Truscott looked over to her husband and suggested that they might take him with them to the rectory where it would be more convenient to discuss his problem. 'We are on our way home. Why don't you come along and take a cup of tea with us?'

Scarcely able to hide his feeling of disappointment, he gladly accepted their invitation. Arriving at the rectory, one of The Park's lesser residences, Rolf followed them inside, passing through an oak panelled hallway into a small, comfortable sitting-room.

Before sitting down, Rolf introduced himself and, explaining his connection with the family of Prince Munster, he told them of how he had always dreamed of one day visiting the place where his grandfather had spent so much of his childhood days. While tea was being prepared, Mr Truscott excused himself and went into his study, returning a few minutes later clutching some books which he spread out on a low table.

Each of the books contained interesting items on the

early history of Maresfield Park, but nothing more recent than the late nineteenth century. One book contained extracts from old newspapers, and from these, he read of occasional visits to The Park of the great Duke of Wellington at the time when it was occupied by Lady Shelley. There was also brief mention of a visit made by Queen Victoria, but all these things had taken place long before Grandfather's time.

Over tea, the rector told Rolf as much as he knew of the more recent history of The Park. He explained that the mansion house had been demolished in the mid 1920s. It had been a large, rambling house, and parts of it were still to be seen incorporated in houses built around the year 1926. More recently other houses, of more modest design had been built. Of Prince Munster, there was nothing the rector could tell Rolf which he did not already know.

'There are,' the rector said, 'quite a number of elderly folk still living in the village, whose parents were in his service. I've no doubt some of them could be persuaded to recollect a few of the anecdotes that have undoubtedly been passed on to them. One dear old lady, Mrs Prewett, who is ninety-four, actually worked at the mansion, and it is quite possible that she may even have known your grandfather. If you care to call here around three o'clock tomorrow afternoon, I can take you along to meet her.'

The rector's offer was gratefully accepted, and thanking the Truscotts for their kindness, Rolf retraced his footsteps to The Chequers.

2

Arriving at *The Chequers*, Rolf was greeted at the door by the landlord, in a more jovial mood than on their first encounter.

'I'm sorry I was a little hasty in refusing you a room, but I really thought we were full. I hope you'll be comfortable with us, and, if you will, we'd like you to share a meal with us this evening. Will eight o'clock suit you?'

Rolf appreciated the offer as there was no other place in the village where he could eat, and Sunday evening was not the time to be foraging for food.

Pat Broxon proved to be a first-rate cook, and she provided an excellent meal. The roast beef was as succulent as any Rolf had ever tasted, and her Yorkshire puddings couldn't have been better if she had been born in Yorkshire. They were able to enjoy a relaxing evening as there was very little activity in the bar, and Charles was content to leave Nancy to cope with the early evening trade. A capable girl in her early twenties, she was totally immune to the banter of the regular customers. Her auburn hair fell in soft ringlets to her shoulders and she had a delightful dimple in her cheeks which showed up when she smiled.

Many of the local lads had tried to persuade Nancy to walk out with them on her day off, but she had eyes only for Ted, and he was a soldier serving in Germany. Ted was the Broxons' only son, and they were happy to know that, one day, Nancy would be a member of the family.

Over coffee, Rolf confided a little of his motive in coming to Maresfield. He told them of his family's connection with the Munsters, and that his grandfather, Karl Muller, had been a frequent visitor during his childhood and had fired his youthful imagination with a

16

desire to see the great estate in England.

'Today,' he said, 'has been a sad day for me; although it was perhaps foolish to expect that everything would be the same today as it once was. My grandfather used to weave such magic into the stories he told over and over again, and I felt I knew every stick and stone on the estate, as well as every tree. Now, alas, all those trees are gone.'

'Not every tree,' interposed Charles, 'in fact there must be hundreds of them left. Some of the larger properties have trees which are well over a hundred years old.'

'Would there be oaks among them?' Rolf asked casually.

'I should think they are mostly oaks' replied Charles.

Rolf wondered silently what he might do in order to see these trees, but he was careful to avoid divulging the precise nature of his mission.

In an endeavour to brighten up the conversation, Charles Broxon asked, 'Do you ride?'

'Yes I do' replied Rolf, 'it is my favourite recreation. Is it possible to hire a horse here in Maresfield?'

'It is indeed! Would you like me to arrange it for you?'

Rolf was pleased for him to do so and, hesitating a moment, asked, 'Do you think that maybe it could be arranged for tomorrow?'

'I'm sure that shouldn't be too difficult to fix,' said Charles, 'I'll introduce you to Chris Charnford, he's almost certain to call in some time during the evening. Chris's father runs the livery stable just along the road from here.'

After serving the menfolk with coffee, Pat Broxon disappeared in the direction of the bar, returning a few minutes later with a tall young man, the man Rolf had seen talking to Charles Broxon earlier in the day. As he entered, Charles jumped to his feet and greeted him with a hearty, 'Hello Chris, we've just been talking about you. I'd like you to meet Rolf Muller. Rolf, this is Chris Charnford.' They shook hands, and Chris, with difficulty, suppressed a smile as Rolf made a formal bow of the head. The three sat down and Pat Broxon brought an extra coffee cup for Chris, and handed a decanter of cognac to her husband.

'By the way Rolf,' Charles said, 'I trust you have no objection to being called by your first name.'

'Not at all! I am honoured.'

'Rolf is staying with us for a couple of weeks,' Charles said to Chris. 'He is very keen to do some riding. I told him you might be able to help.'

'But of course, I'm sure we'll be able to fix you up,' Chris said.

'Have you done much riding?'

'Yes,' Rolf replied, 'back home in Germany I ride on every possible occasion. I have my own horse.'

The three men spent a very pleasant evening together, and Rolf, explaining to Chris the predicament he was in, was assured by him that anything he could do to make his stay in Maresfield as pleasant as possible, he would do willingly. Roif took an immediate liking to Chris and when the young Englishman suggested that they might both go riding together, he fairly beamed at the prospect.

It was eleven o'clock before the party broke up and Rolf made his way up to his room. Before retiring for the night he took from his pocket a notebook he had brought with him in order to log his visit to England. On the front page he noted that this had been a day of mixed blessings.

3

Monday morning dawned. Dressed and shaved, Rolf descended the two flights of stairs and was shown by Mrs Broxon into the breakfast room. A morning paper was put into his hand, and he was assured that breakfast would be ready in ten minutes. From the direction of the kitchen came the sizzling sound of bacon on the grill and the aroma of coffee. Within five minutes Pat Broxon returned, bringing with her packets of cereals and telling Rolf, 'If you'll take what you want of these, the rest will be along by the time you're ready.' The rest, when it came, consisted of two rashers of bacon, two fried eggs, grilled tomatoes and mushrooms.

'Will you have tea or coffee?'

He had earlier thought of requesting tea, but the wonderful smell of the percolated coffee prompted him to say, 'Coffee will be fine.'

Rolf had no difficulty in finding his way to the Charnford farm, and when he drove into the stable yard, Chris Charnford was already leading out two fine looking chestnut geldings saddled and ready to be off. He hailed Rolf with a cheery, 'Hello there' and then he introduced him to Rupert, his mount for the day. Approaching Rupert very gently, he let the horse take stock of him. A soft word or two and then he gently patted and stroked him. Leading him by the reins, Rolf walked him a few times round the stable yard, all the time talking softly, establishing a relationship and mutual trust. Chris was pleased with the approach, and recognised a true horseman.

Together the two men mounted and walked their horses out into the lane, turning towards the heathland at the southernmost end of the Ashdown Forest. Skirting

Fairwarp village, they began to climb the gentle slope towards the hamlet of Duddleswell, where they left the roadway and joined an old bridleway leading across open forest towards Nutley village. This bridle path meandered over a wide expanse of bracken and heather, with here and there patches of gorse, its yellow flowers bedecked with gossamer shimmering in the early morning sunlight. As yet, there was no real heat in the sun, but the sky overhead was blue and cloudless, and soaring high above a skylark was singing, heralding the dawn of a new day.

The two men rode silently side by side, but from time to time Chris would break the silence to point out interesting landmarks. They neared a small enclosure surrounded by a low stone wall, and as they approached, Chris told Rolf that this was known locally as the Airman's Grave. It consisted of a tiny garden with a cross in the centre marking the spot where six airmen had lost their lives during the war, when their bomber plane had crashed. The mother of one of the members of the crew had erected the memorial in his memory. Pointing with his finger to where the heathland rose and fell at regular intervals, Chris said, 'You see those mounds over there. Apparently there were twelve regiments of soldiers camped here about two hundred years ago, and these hillocks are said to be the site of their field kitchens.'

They moved on and, coming to another bridleway, they took a right turning and instead of going on towards Nutley they made for a more northerly point in the open country. At first they continued to trot quietly, Chris leading the way. As the going became easier, he changed into a canter. Looking over his shoulder, and seeing the eager look in Rolf's eye, he called back to him, 'Do you see that clump of trees straight ahead of you, on the horizon? Let's make a race of it!'

Rolf needed no second bidding. Drawing up alongside he shouted, 'Good, let's go!'

They set off at full gallop. For the first two hundred yards or so they rode neck and neck, the two horses, manes flying, eyes flashing, thrilled at the opportunity to show their mettle. This was truly exhilarating, each combination of horse and rider so well matched, and it was not until they were within twenty yards of their goal that Chris's mount pulled ahead, finishing less than half a length in front of his rival. When they came to a halt, Rolf leaned over and clasped the hand of his companion and, shaking it vigorously he said, 'That was wonderful. I have never before had such competition. You are a fine horseman, Chris.'

'You're pretty good yourself,' replied Chris, 'particularly as you're riding a strange horse.'

Going at a walking pace, they continued for a short time before they saw in the distance another horseman. As they drew closer, Chris recognised the rider as Sir Harold Grantwell and the grey horse as Peggy, a gentle eight year old mare from his father's stable.

Sir Harold was a large, heavily built man. It was questionable as to whether he actually enjoyed riding, or was doing it because it was the done thing. No horse other than Peggy would have tolerated his awkwardness in the saddle. Given the choice, Chris would have avoided meeting him and was prepared for the possibility of being ignored by Grantwell, but this morning he was to be favoured with a word from him.

'Good day to you, Charnford,' the man called out as they drew alongside him.

'Good day, Sir Harold' Chris replied. 'May I introduce my friend Rolf Muller. Rolf, this is Sir Harold Grantwell.'

Sir Harold made no attempt to shake hands, but nodded briefly.

'Living in these parts, are you?' he queried.

Chris noticed a look of distaste on the older man's face.

'No, Sir Harold,' Rolf replied. 'Just visiting.'

With a further curt 'good day' Grantwell rode off and was soon out of sight.

The two continued in silence side by side. All the zest for riding appeared to have left them, particularly so with Chris. He seemed preoccupied. After some time he said, 'That man fairly makes my blood boil with his damned arrogance. The countryside around here is fast becoming littered with his type. They make a pile of money in the city and then buy their way into the country, grabbing all the best properties and as much land as they can lay hands on, and good honest country folk who've given the best years of their lives to the land, are unable to afford the price of the cottages they live in.'

There was nothing Rolf could say in reply, so he kept silent and was not sorry when they were back at the stables.

He lost no time in returning to The Chequers where he bought himself a beer and sandwiches before going up to his room to prepare for his afternoon's visit to the rector. There were at least two hours to spare before he needed to leave and so, after washing and freshening up, he sat down to write letters, one to his parents and another to his young sister, Helga.

He gave them an account of his fruitless attempt to explore the Maresfield Park estate, telling them that it was no longer the vast open expanse that his grandfather had remembered. It seemed that his mission was a failure, but he would not be returning immediately to Germany. What he had seen of England he liked, and he had been encouraged by the friendliness of the people he had met. There was no particular reason for him to hurry back home, and he had decided to stay for at least a couple of weeks. The countryside around Maresfield offered good riding facilities, and he had comfortable accommodation at the village inn.

By the time he had finished writing it was almost three o'clock, and so he took a brisk walk along to the rectory. Mr Truscott was waiting at his garden gate, and he suggested that they should walk to Mrs Prewett's cottage on the far side of the village. He had a call to make on the way and, arriving at the village stores, he invited Rolf to go inside with him to meet the grocer, George Turley.

'I'll warn you,' said the rector, 'Mr Turley is a frightful gossip, and you may find it difficult to get away.'

Rolf's first impression of the man was not particularly favourable. In his late fifties, his face lean and long, he had two small beady eyes which darted to and fro, reminding Rolf of a squirrel. His nose was slightly hooked, and a pair of rimless spectacles balanced precariously on the end of it.

In spite of this, the grocer managed to project a degree of affability when the rector made his introduction, and before shaking hands he made sure that his own were clean by rubbing them on the spotless white apron he was wearing.

4

George was delighted to meet the tall, aristocratic looking young man and for once was pleased that there were no other customers in the shop. A stranger staying in the village was always a useful subject for conversation, and to have first-hand knowledge of who he was, and what he was about would indeed be a feather in the Turley cap. He tried desperately to extract from Rolf as much detail as possible of his purpose for being in Maresfield, but all he could elicit was that he was taking an extended holiday in order to improve his English. Try as he might, George could get nothing more out of him, and so he was left to allow his imagination to conceive a reason for the young German's visit.

When Rolf and the rector departed, the shopkeeper tried hard to concentrate on the task of tidying his shelves, but every now and again he would pause, scratch his head and ponder: 'I wonder! His English is perfect already. Why should he come to Maresfield? It's not exactly on the tourist map. He's staying at The Chequers. He's friendly with the rector. I hope Mrs Broxon comes in this afternoon; she often comes in on a Monday afternoon.' It was no use; he just could not settle down to do anything more, and was about to ask his wife to come and take over when the door opened and a customer came in. It was Pat Broxon.

'Good morning, Mrs Broxon; what a pleasant surprise. How very kind of you to drop in!'

The landlady of the village inn was clearly taken aback by the profuse and totally unexpected welcome. Her occasional patronage of the village shop was purely a matter of convenience, and it was common knowledge that George Turley strongly disapproved of public houses in general, and *The Chequers* in particular.

'What can I do for you today?' asked Mr Turley.

She handed him a list of items and he busied himself with her order, from time to time murmuring pleasantries about the weather, and other trivia.

When he had completed the order and placed the cash safely in the till he observed, 'I had one of your guests in the shop a short time ago. What a remarkable young man he is. Such fine breeding. He told me quite a lot about himself.'

Mrs Broxon was not accustomed to discussing her guests with other people, but she was so overcome by Mr Turley's new-found geniality that she was temporarily taken off guard, and revealed to him the fact that Mr Muller was distantly related to the family of Prince Munster. She immediately regretted the indiscretion, and said to the grocer, 'I must ask you to keep it to yourself, Mr Turley.'

'But of course, Mrs Broxon,' he replied, 'I shall most certainly respect your confidence.'

Mrs Broxon having departed, George Turley called out for his wife to come through to the shop. She noticed the look of excitement on his face as she asked him, 'What is it, George?'

'Oh, Edith you'll never guess. I've just had a German nobleman in the shop. The rector brought him in especially to introduce me to him. He's the grandson of Prince Munster and he's staying at *The Chequers*. He must be either a count or a baron.'

The rector and his companion continued their walk in silence and soon arrived at a trim little cottage standing by the roadside. It had a neatly kept garden with white and red roses on either side of the pathway. Tapping gently on the door which was slightly ajar, the rector called out,

'Mrs Prewett, may I come in?'

The old lady was expecting him. It was his usual time. 'Come straight in, Rector; the door is open.'

Sitting in a comfortable easy chair was an old lady with hair as white as snow, and light blue eyes which lit up with joy as the rector leaned over to shake her hand.

'I've brought someone to see you, Mrs Prewett. This is a

gentleman from Germany who is staying for a holiday in the village; Mr Rolf Muller.' Rolf shook the old lady by the hand and accepted a chair. There was a long silence which was broken eventually by Mrs Prewett. Her voice quavered as she spoke.

'I've never been to Germany. George promised me that we should go one day, but we never seemed to be able to save enough money. Now he's gone, rest his soul, and we shall never go. We both worked for Prince Munster up the The Park, you know. George was coachman right up to the time war broke out; the first war, that is. I worked there as a chambermaid some of the time, and sometimes, when Master Paul and Master Frederick were on holiday, I looked after them.'

Rolf sat forward on the edge of his seat and was about to say something, but the old lady continued, 'It was through having to look after the boys that I first met my George. When we went for picnics or on outings to the seaside, Prewett used to take us in the brake.'

Mrs Prewett paused for breath, and unable to contain himself further, Rolf blurted out, 'Tell me please, are you Kitty?'

Startled, she could only murmur a scarcely audible 'Yes.'

Rolf continued, 'Do you remember a little boy named Karl?'

A far away look came into the old lady's eyes; again they began to light up, and a beautiful, wistful smile appeared on the wrinkled cheeks. 'Oh yes, I do; such a beautiful boy. Karl and his father used to bring the boys over at holiday time.'

'He was my grandfather,' said Rolf.

Old Kitty suddenly became young Kitty; she looked searchingly into his face and said, 'I should have known. You are so much as I imagined he would be when he was grown up, but if you know my name, he must have talked about me.'

'Kitty, he remembered you until the day he died. He told me many wonderful things of his holidays at Maresfield Park, and always he would talk about your kindness. It is such a pleasure for me that I should at last meet you.'

The rector was quite content to leave the two of them to talk together, but at last, sensing that the old lady was beginning to tire, he wisely said, 'Perhaps we ought to be going.'

Just as he said this, the front door opened and a young lady came in, calling out as she entered, 'It's Kitty, Granny.'

With no more than a nod to the two men she went over to her grandmother and lovingly putting her arms around her, kissed her on the cheek, causing the old lady to beam with joy.

'Oh Kitty,' the old lady said, 'this gentleman has come from Germany to see me. Will you introduce them Rector, please?'

With a humorously affected formality he said, 'Miss Glover, may I present Herr Rolf Muller. Mr Muller, this is Miss Catherine Glover.'

As they shook hands, Rolf could see in the face opposite him the image of what Kitty Prewett must have been when she was her grand-daughter's age. Seeing a puzzled look on Rolf's face, the young lady hastened to explain,

'My parents named me Catherine, but Grandpa always called me Kitty because, he said, I was so much like Granny, and the name has stuck.'

Before the visitors departed, Rolf was given a pressing invitation to call again the following afternoon to take tea with the old lady; an invitation which he had no hesitation in accepting.

As they walked slowly back towards the village the rector said, 'George Prewett had already died before I came to Maresfield. They had a son, Albert who was killed in North Africa during the war, and a daughter, Connie. Connie married a young Royal Engineers officer, Raymond Glover. He's an architect, with an office in Brighton. They live up in The Park. Kitty's their only child.'

Most of what the rector said was completely lost on the young German. How wonderful that he had actually met someone who had known his grandfather, and how extraordinary that it should be Kitty. Tomorrow he would see her again; yes, grandfather would have approved.

Arriving at The Chequers, Rolf said goodbye to the rector, thanking him profusely for the introduction he had effected, and promised that he would call again at the rectory quite soon.

5

Rolf went up to his room, washed and changed ready for going out for the evening, when there was a gentle tap on his door. He opened it, and was confronted by Alice, the Broxons' daily help. 'Excuse me, sir,' she said, 'there's a telephone call for you.'

He hurried down to the reception desk, puzzled and wondering who could be calling him. He picked up the phone and said, 'Rolf Muller.'

'Oh Rolf, Chris Charnford here. I'm glad I caught you. I've just been thinking; if you're not doing anything special this evening, why don't we have a run out somewhere? We could perhaps go into Eastbourne, have a meal, and then take a look at a bit of the coastline. What do you say?'

'I say yes, Chris. It sounds like a very good idea. I have to eat somewhere.'

'When can you be ready?'

'I'm ready now,' Rolf said. 'I was just about to go out when you rang.'

'Then come round and I'll introduce you to the family. They'd like to meet you.'

The family comprised parents, Arthur and Sylvia, their daughter Daphne, and Chris. When Rolf arrived he was met at the door by Mrs Charnford who greeted him with a warm smile of welcome. Reaching out her hand she said, 'You must be Mr Muller. I'm Christopher's mother, Sylvia Charnford.'

'I'm delighted to meet you, Mrs Charnford,' said Rolf. He was shown into a cozy sitting-room where Mr Charnford was rising from his seat.

'Arthur, this is Mr Muller.' Sylvia beamed.

'Glad to met you, Mr Muller. Do sit down, Chris won't

be long. Did you enjoy your ride this morning?'

'Oh, thank you, yes. It was wonderful. The countryside is so beautiful, and so interesting. And what a fine horse Chris gave me to ride.'

'Yes, Chris told me you had Rupert. In my opinion he's the finest horse in the stable, though Chris swears by his own horse, Vincent.'

'Chris is a fine horseman, Mr Charnford.'

'Yes, he is,' Arthur said with a touch of pride, 'but apparently you are no mean performer yourself . . .'

The conversation was interrupted by Chris coming into the room. 'Sorry I wasn't down to meet you, Rolf, but I'm sure you've managed to introduce yourself.'

His mother said, 'It's all right, Chris, I'm sure Mr Muller will excuse our informality.'

'But of course, Mrs Charnford. You are kind to receive me, a stranger, into your home.'

'Where's Daphne?' Chris asked his mother.

'She's in her room, getting ready to go out. Kitty's calling for her in about half an hour.'

Rolf noticed that when his mother said who was coming for Daphne, there was a wistful look on Chris's face, and quite suddenly he settled himself into an easy chair, no longer in any particular hurry to be going.

'Will you have a cup of tea, Mr Muller?' Mrs Charnford asked. Rolf was just about to decline when Chris interposed, 'Yes, I'm sure he will, Mother, I'd like one too.'

Turning to his father, Chris opened up a conversation explaining Rolf's particular interest in Maresfield Park, and of the young man's kinship with Prince Munster. Tea was brought in, not by Mrs Charnford, but by a most attractive, deliciously beautiful girl such as Rolf had never seen in his whole life. He rose dreamily from his seat as the girl set down the tea tray. He was stunned, weak, totally unprepared for the vision now confronting him. Why hadn't Chris warned him? Certainly he had mentioned having a little sister, but this; this was no little sister; this was an angel.

Vaguely, as if at a great distance, he heard: 'Rolf, this is my sister Daphne - Daphne, this is Rolf Muller.' He took the outstretched hand gently, reverently, and with a voice which he did not recognise as his own, murmured simply, 'How do you do?'

'Hello, Mr Muller.'

She laughed gaily as she said it, her voice sounding like the tinkling of sleigh-bells.

'May I have my hand back, please.'

'Oh, I'm sorry,' he whispered, full of confusion. Mrs Charnford relieved the situation by saying to Rolf, 'Please do sit down,' and to Daphne she said, 'Will you pour the tea, dear?'

It was almost five minutes before Rolf was sufficiently composed to take his first sip of tea, and Daphne, sensing his embarrassment, attempted to put him at his ease. 'I understand you have already met my friend Kitty.'

He replied, 'Oh yes; Kitty Glover you mean? I called on her grandmother, Mrs Prewett, this afternoon along with the Reverend Mr Truscott, and Miss Glover was also visiting.'

'My word, Daph,' Chris interrupted, 'the grapevine's been working overtime.'

'Oh, you!' Daphne retorted meaningfully, and to Rolf she said, 'You'll be meeting her again shortly.'

There was the sound of a vehicle coming to a halt in front of the house and, glancing through the window, Mrs Charnford saw Kitty's bright red little two-seater Spitfire drawing up alongside Rolf's blue Mercedes.

'Here's Kitty now,' she said.

Daphne ran out to meet her friend, and it was some ten minutes or so before the two girls came in to join the others.

'Hello,' said Kitty, taking in the group with the single word of greeting.

Daphne followed up with, 'You've already met Mr Muller.'

After a few minutes Mrs. Charnford asked, 'How is your grandmother, Kitty?'

'Oh she's fine, and so excited at having met Mr Muller today. She's quite sure that he's come to England specially to meet her.'

'Perhaps,' said Rolf, 'the next time I come to Maresfield

it may be to see her. She is very special, and it has been a
privilege to meet her.'

'Don't forget, you are coming to see her again
tomorrow,' she reminded him.

'How could I?' he chuckled. 'Will you also be there?'

'Possibly, either mother or myself.'

Chris sat quietly in a corner. An idea was forming itself
in his mind. Looking over at his sister, he asked her, 'If
you're not doing anything special tonight, why don't we
all go out together?'

Before replying, Daphne turned towards her friend
and, seeing no sign of objection, she asked her brother,
'What have you in mind?'

'I thought of taking Rolf to The Rose Garden.' He
explained to Rolf, 'It's a great little eating place where
they do some wonderful home style cooking. If it suits
everybody, I'll phone through and see if they've got a
table for us.'

While he was telephoning, Daphne asked Rolf, 'Are
you quite happy about this Mr Muller? We seem to be
intruding.'

'Of course, I'm very happy,' he replied with a smile,
'and please call me Rolf.'

Chris came back to tell them that he'd been able to book
a table for four, and they prepared to leave for the short
drive to the South Downs.

Taking leave of Mr and Mrs Charnford, the girls took
their places in the back of the Mercedes, and Chris
climbed in alongside Rolf. They took the Eastbourne
road, driving steadily through Maresfield village and on
into Uckfield where they were held up for some minutes
at the railway crossing.

Glancing in his driving mirror, Rolf caught a glimpse of
Daphne, and without realising it he continued to gaze at
some length. Eventually the train made its way out of the
station and the crossing gates were opened, but Rolf
made no attempt to start the car until the sound of
hooters coming from behind roused him from his reverie.

'Feeling tired old chap?' Chris asked.

Rolf apologised sheepishly, and the car moved on up
the hill through the old town and out into the country.

The girls chatted away to each other while Chris pointed out various landmarks along the route. Taking a sharp right turn through East Hoathly and on through Golden Cross, they joined the dual carriageway which eventually took them into Polegate. There, they abandoned the Eastbourne road and turned right along a road leading towards the South Downs. Meandering through a series of delightful little Sussex hamlets with flintstone cottages and gardens filled with old-fashioned English flowers, they drove on through leafy lanes until they came at last to a narrow driveway at the entrance of which was a small discreet sign indicating that The Rose Garden Restaurant was down to the right at a distance of half a mile.

Rolf had been intrigued when he first heard the name of the restaurant, but now, as he approached it, he understood why it had been so called; there were all kinds of roses everywhere he looked, but around the doors and windows were masses of pink ramblers; a glorious sight.

They parked the car and walked towards the cottage restaurant. As they entered they were enchanted by the subtle fragrance. The proprietor met them at the door, and he conducted them to a cosy little cocktail bar where they were invited to sit and take an aperitif. They were each given a menu to study but it was left to Chris to select the meal. On a previous visit he had enjoyed a breast of chicken with crab, and this he strongly recommended. He ordered a bottle of medium white house wine which previous experience had proved to be a delightful accompaniment to the food.

The restaurant itself was quite small, with no more than a dozen tables. They were shown to a table set in an alcove, and this afforded them a certain amount of privacy. There was still quite a lot of daylight, and from where they sat they were able to watch the bees making their brief excursions from flower to flower.

The food this evening was even more tempting than Chris had remembered it; Rolf congratulated him on his choice of wine, although, as Chris pointed out, it was usually safe to have the wine of the house, as the restaurant's reputation depended on it. The girls were nearest the window and were able to see further out on to the lawn. Daphne, who was sitting beside Rolf, leaned over and touched him gently on the sleeve and said, 'Oh look at that little rabbit over there.'

Taken by surprise, Rolf turned his head rather quickly, and as he did so, Daphne's hair brushed against his cheek. He didn't see the rabbit. By the time his glance was directed towards the window it was gone, but it had unwittingly played a significant part in his life. He was stunned; confused, utterly bewildered. What was happening? No, this was impossible; it couldn't be. He had never before felt like this; he was hopelessly in love.

The hors d'oeuvre trolley was brought to their table, and the others had made their selection by the time Rolf had composed himself. With an effort he turned his attention to the food, and they were able to start their meal. Chris engaged Kitty in conversation, and from time to time Daphne would turn to Rolf and reward him with a brief gentle smile, and a word or two of small talk concerning the merits of the food. If she had any suspicion of Rolf's predicament, she was careful to conceal it.

By the time the meal was over, Chris and Kitty had discovered that they had a number of things in common. In the past Chris had always thought of her as a rather special chum of his sister, growing year by year into an attractive young lady, but somehow, this evening he was seeing her in a different light. Was it the scent of the roses, or the subtle fragrance of the perfume she was wearing? No; it was more than that; it was something as old as the hills. Kitty had long been aware of Chris, and Daphne had often teased her for what had been a schoolgirl crush, and so she had been careful to hide any sign of interest she may have had in him.

The evening was still young when they left the restaurant, so they drove on to Birling Gap. Leaving the car in one of the roadside parking bays, they took a footpath leading over the clifftops towards Beachy Head, which, Chris mentioned, was the highest of the many cliffs on the south coast. Chris and Kitty walked on ahead and Daphne assumed the role of guide, giving Rolf the benefit of her vast knowledge of the surrounding countryside. At one point the footpath came quite close to the edge of the cliff, and they were able to look down on the calm sea some five hundred feet or so below. The fading sun, slowly disappearing over the horizon and casting its last shimmering rays over the water, created a backcloth for the lighthouse standing in sharp relief on the rocks below.

Daphne, looking ahead to where the others walked on, experienced a sudden feeling of pleasure as she saw that Chris and Kitty were holding hands; somehow it seemed so right. By the time they returned to the car it was quite dark, and they decided to take a shorter route home rather than the scenic one. The journey to Maresfield took no more than half an hour, and was completed in total silence. When they reached the entrance to The Park, Chris asked Rolf to stop the car, and he and Kitty got out to walk the short distance to Holmwood.

Rolf drove on until he arrived at Charnford's. Bringing the car to a halt, he quickly got out and sprang to the rear door, but Daphne was already out before he had a chance to open it. She turned to shake his hand and said, 'Goodnight, Rolf. Thank you so much for a lovely evening.'

Before he could reply, she was gone, and as the house door was closing behind her, he managed to murmur, 'Goodnight, Daphne.'

There was so much he wanted to say; his mind was in a turmoil. He sat motionless in the car for some time, hoping that she might come back and give him the opportunity to ask if he could see her again. In despair he gave up and drove back to The Chequers. There were only three customers in the bar, but Rolf found some consolation in the welcome he was given. It was Nancy's evening off, and Charles Broxon was serving behind the bar.

'What will you have, Rolf?' he asked.

'A lager, please, and perhaps these gentlemen will join me.' Drinks were served, and a place was made for Rolf at the table where the three were sitting. It was not long before Charles Broxon himself came to join them, and he introduced the three locals to his guest. They were Martin Bell, Stan Croft and Alf Williams.

Stan Croft, the village postman, was sorry he had to be going after his drink was finished, as he would need to be up early in the morning. Alf Williams, who was senior mechanic at the local garage, would also need to be following, but before he left he insisted on buying a reciprocal glass of lager for the young gentleman. Martin Bell was retired and so had no urgent reason for being early to bed. Charles explained to Rolf that Martin was a sidesman at the church; he had formerly been the village blacksmith, but the smithy had been closed down for almost two years.

When Stan Croft and Alf Williams took their leave, Charles busied himself behind the bar, leaving Rolf to chat with the old blacksmith.

'My family were in the smithy for over a hundred years,' Martin said proudly. 'My grandfather started it in 1875 when he was twenty-five years old. How times have changed. My father used to help him to shoe as many as forty horses in a day during the first war; that was until Father had to go into the army as a farrier.'

Returning to the table, Charles remarked to Rolf, 'Martin's father must have done a lot of work for Prince Munster in his time.'

'He certainly did,' Martin said. 'From what he told me, the Prince must have kept a very large stable.'

Rolf asked him, 'Has your father been a long time dead?'

'Dead? He's not dead! Whatever gave you the idea he was dead?'

Martin appeared to be upset, and Rolf hastened to apologise.

'I'm so sorry. How stupid of me!'

Seeing Rolf's distress, Martin chuckled, 'Don't worry; he's got a lot of life in him yet.'

Much to Martin's surprise, Rolf said, 'I'd very much like to meet him. It's just possible that he may have known my grandfather. Could you arrange it for me?'

'Oh, that'll be no trouble; he's living at Rockwood, the old people's home on the London Road. I shall be going to see him tomorrow morning. You're welcome to come with me.'

It was arranged that Martin would be at *The Chequers* at half past ten the next morning.

6

As they walked along the middle drive, turning into the gateway of Holmwood, Kitty said, 'It's been a lovely evening, Chris; thank you so much.'

'No, Kitty; thank you for making it such a perfect evening.'

They stopped walking, and stood gazing into each other's eyes. For a long time they lingered, just looking, as if searching for something. Neither of them was willing to spoil the magic of this precious moment by uttering an inappropriate word. They both knew what their hearts wanted to say, but was this the time to say it? It was the very first time they had been close to each other, and although Chris knew for a certainty that he was in love with Kitty, he was conscious that this had all happened during this one evening together.

He had never felt this way with any other girl, and he longed to take her in his arms, to kiss those beautiful lips which tonight he had noticed for the first time. If only he had known how much Kitty wanted him to kiss her. She had no doubt in her mind; how had she managed to hide it all this time? There could never be any other man in her life. He was a man in every way; strong, sincere, not a ladies' man; but her man.

They were suddenly brought down to earth by the headlights of a car turning into the drive. Kitty's father and mother were returning home after an evening out. Coming to a halt in front of the house, Connie and Raymond came over to where the young couple were standing. Kitty threw her arms round her mother and whispered, 'Oh Mummy, I've had such a wonderful evening.'

Her father, seeing the man standing sheepishly in the

background said, 'Hello, Chris; this is a surprise. Now I know what Kitty means when she says she's going out with Daphne.'

'Oh Daddy!' Kitty blushed exquisitely.

'Come in and have a nightcap,' Raymond invited.

Chris readily accepted the invitation and waited for Raymond to put the car away in the garage. Kitty helped her mother prepare coffee while her father poured brandy for Chris and himself. Raymond said, 'Connie's mother has been telling us about the young German fellow staying in the village. She's full of excitement. He's calling on her again tomorrow afternoon. Connie's going along to give him tea.'

'He's a very likeable chap, Mr Glover,' said Chris. 'As a matter of fact we've been out together this evening, along with Daphne and Kitty. We rode in the forest together this morning. He's a fine horseman.'

'Kitty was saying he's somehow connected with Prince Munster,' Raymond continued.

'Yes; he came over here hoping to see The Park. It's been a bitter disappointment to him.'

'It was before my time, of course,' said Raymond, 'but my partner's uncle had a hand in the development of the estate. He has lots of old plans and photographs which might be of interest to the young fellow. I'll have them sent over sometime tomorrow.'

They chatted amiably for half an hour before Chris decided he ought to be going. He thanked Mr and Mrs Glover for their hospitality, and Kitty accompanied him to the door.

'When can I see you again, Kitty?' Chris asked.

'Do you really want to, Chris, or are you just being polite?' Kitty teased.

'I really want to see you, very soon.'

There was no doubting his sincerity. She looked into his eyes for confirmation of what she thought she heard. There was no mistake; he drew her firmly into his embrace; their lips sought each other and they kissed long and tenderly.

'Oh Chris,' she said, 'I do love you.'

'I'll ring you tomorrow and we'll arrange something,'

Chris promised.

'Make it soon, dear,' she said, and, reluctantly, they parted.

Chris began to walk home, a mere half mile, but whatever the distance, it meant nothing. It was a clear moonlight night with a million stars looking down on an enchanted footpath bordered on either side with wild roses. He had never before realised that Paradise was so near to home.

When he arrived home his sister was curled up in an easy chair, her parents having already retired for the night.

'Well?' she said quizically.

Chris made no response, so she got up from her seat and playfully snapped her fingers in front of his eyes saying, 'Are you awake, brother?'

He composed himself and said, 'Oh, hello Daph. Not in bed yet?'

'No,' she retorted, 'as you may or may not see, I am not in bed. But never mind about me. What kept you so long? Don't keep me in suspense.'

'Oh,' Chris replied casually, 'Kitty's parents arrived home at the same time as we did, and they invited me in for coffee. What about you. Didn't you ask Rolf in?'

'Really brother!' she responded with mock horror, 'a girl has her reputation to consider,' and then, 'I like him, Chris; he's awfully good-looking.'

'Are you seeing him again?' Chris asked her.

'I don't suppose so, but it would be rather nice if we could all go out together again sometime.'

Chris went silent for a moment before blurting out, 'I'm taking Kitty out, just the two of us. I hope you don't mind, but I think she loves me.'

'Oh you idiot; I could have told you that years ago. Oh Chris,' she whispered, 'I'm so thrilled. And do you love her?'

'Oh yes,' he said fervently, 'I do love her.'

A surge of pleasure suddenly came over Daphne. She was like a mother hen; her very best friend and her brother were in love; she wanted to ask all sorts of questions, but no; she would be patient. Tomorrow she would make a point of seeing Kitty. It would be so much more romantic coming from her; you could never get any sort of sense from a brother.

'I'll be off to bed then,' she called out to Chris, and humming a little tune, she dreamily went off to her room, a look of quiet satisfaction on her face.

7

His parents were already having their breakfast when Chris came back into the house, having set the men to work in the stables. Feeling hungry, he was glad to sit down to a generous helping of eggs, bacon and sausages.

'Daphne not up yet?' he asked his mother.

'No dear,' she replied, 'I don't suppose we shall see her much before ten o'clock. You boys must have kept her out late.'

Chris made no response; his mother was fishing, and he wasn't going to get hooked. Instead, he said to his father, 'I'm going up to town shortly, Dad. Is there anything I can do for you?'

'If you're going to be anywhere near Piccadilly Circus perhaps you can call in at Simpsons and see if they have any of those socks like the ones your mother bought for me last Christmas. You can get me a couple of pairs.'

Kitty woke early; she dressed and joined her parents at breakfast. After she had finished she walked towards the French windows leading to the garden. Turning to her mother she said, 'Mummy, I'm going to pick a few roses. If anyone phones me will you give me a shout please.'

Twenty minutes later she returned to the house. There had been no call; she tried to hide her disappointment, but it didn't go unnoticed. Connie tactfully avoided making any reference to her daughter's distress, and asked her, 'Will you be coming to Granny's with me this afternoon?'

Kitty said she thought not, but was spared from offering a reason; the telephone rang, and she almost ran to answer it.

'Hello,' she said breathlessly, 'this is Kitty Glover.'

The tone of her voice changed; 'Oh, hello Daphne. I was half expecting a call from Chris.' There was a pause, and then, 'All right. I'll be over in half an hour.'

She spent twenty minutes or so making herself ready for going out and then went to the garage to get her car out. As she was reversing onto the drive, her mother came out of the house.

'There's another call for you, Kitty.'

Kitty came back into the hall and took the telephone in her hand. 'Kitty Glover,' she said. 'Chris ... where are you? Daphne said you'd gone to London.'

She listened in silence as Chris explained that he was paying an annual visit for a dental check-up, and could he call for her at eight o'clock this evening?

'Yes, of course,' she answered. 'Goodbye, darling.'

As Kitty drove up to the Charnford house, Daphne heard the car and ran out to meet her. Together they walked to the rear of the house, across the lawn to the summerhouse.

'Chris phoned me from Haywards Heath station just after I'd spoken to you,' said Kitty. 'He had to rush off quickly as his train was coming in. Sorry I was off-hand with you, Daphne, when you called. I didn't mean to be.'

'Think nothing of it, my pet. I quite understand. Now tell me all about it.'

Kitty assumed an air of mystery; she tried to channel the conversation away from herself by asking,

'What did you think of Rolf? Did you mind being left alone with him?'

'Come on, Kitty,' Daphne parried. 'Let's talk about you. Rolf is very nice; no, I didn't mind being alone with him; he's a perfect gentlemen. Now, to the serious business. My brother came home all dewy eyed and sentimental; I couldn't get any sense out of him. Mother tells me he went off in a daze this morning, and you, my sweet, are looking like the cat that had the cream.'

'I'm seeing him again this evening,' Kitty conceded.

'Did you make any progress with Rolf?'

'Not so far as I'm aware,' replied Daphne, 'but he's good company, and if he was to ask me out again I should probably agree; he's only here for a week or two, so it wouldn't do any harm I suppose.'

'Didn't he suggest anything?' Kitty asked. 'I couldn't help noticing the way he looked at you over dinner. I should say you made quite an impact on him.'

'Well I shan't do any chasing,' said Daphne; 'but it won't be at all difficult for me to be nice to him.'

The two young ladies were in a happy frame of mind when Mrs Charnford came to call them into the house for coffee. She had known just where to find them; ever since they were children together they had gone to the summerhouse when something special had happened or when they had had some childish plans to make. They had been friends for as long as they could remember, having attended the same nursery school and kindergarten, preparatory school and then on to Roedean.

This year they had been thinking in terms of a career, but up to now, nothing definite had been planned other than a course in cordon bleu cooking and it would be six months before that was due to commence.

8

Rolf was descending the stairs as Martin Bell approached the door of The Chequers. Together they went to the rear of the inn where Rolf's car was parked. Martin was impressed by the gleaming Mercedes and was sorry that none of his friends were around to see him getting in alongside the tall, distinguished looking young German.

It took no more than five minutes to reach Rockwood, the old people's home, and in another five they were in a comfortable but small bedsitter where Martin introduced Rolf to his father. One or two personal matters were discussed between father and son before Martin left it to Rolf to explain to the old man who he was, and the reason why he wanted to meet him. The old man was in full possession of all his faculties and it proved to be no problem for him to recall events which had taken place sixty or seventy years ago.

He well remembered the German prince who had lived so long ago at Maresfield Park, although, of course, he had never been privileged to meet him.

'I knew old George Prewett though; he used to bring th' Prince's 'orses down to my old dad to be shod.'

'Did he ever bring any of the Prince's children down with him?' Rolf asked.

'Not s' far as I remember; but I remember one little 'un used to come sometimes. 'E were a German lad; couldn't speak much English. 'E were a grand little lad, though.'

'Was his name Karl?' Rolf asked eagerly.

The old man scratched his head, and eventually said, 'That's right; it were Karl.'

'I'm Karl's grandson,' Rolf said.

An expression of incredulity came onto the face of the old man, but as he looked long and searchingly at his

German visitor his eyes lit up, and something stirred within him. A picture of the little boy from many years back began to form in his mind.

'Do you remember any of the tasks your father performed for the Prince, apart from horse shoeing?' the young man asked.

'Far as I remember, there was only one job, an' I wouldn' 'a remembered 'e 'cept 'twere a real big 'un; 'an didn't we 'ave a rush on; 'twere a big chest we did. Must 'ave weighed nigh on a couple of 'undredweight,' asserted the old man.

Rolf asked him, 'I don't suppose you can remember what it was to be used for?'

'No! 'tweren't none o' my business,' the old man retorted.

Rolf could think of nothing more to say to him, so, shaking him warmly by the hand, and assuring him that he would call on him again within a day or two, he joined Martin who was waiting in the hall outside. Martin returned to the room for a minute or two, and then he accompanied Rolf to the car.

'It was a great pleasure to meet your father,' Rolf said as the car drew away from Rockwood, 'and now, will you do me the favour of taking lunch with me; perhaps you could suggest a suitable place to eat?'

Martin suggested The Peacock. They took a right turn in Nutley village, making towards Piltdown, crossing the Haywards Heath road and on past the Piltdown golf course until they reached The Peacock Inn set back from the road. It proved to be a delightful old inn with oak beams and lattice windows, and over the fireplace it had a beautiful tapestry with a large peacock motif. Rolf had to stoop quite low to get through the doorway.

The restaurant was not open, but they were able to have a bar meal. They both settled for a ploughman's lunch together with a pint of lager. There was an empty table near a window and they took their drinks over to it. As they were waiting to be served the door opened, and a military looking, fresh faced elderly gentleman came in. He nodded to Martin who returned the brief salutation before quietly remarking to Rolf.

'He's Colonel Briggs; lives in The Park; retired regular army.'

The colonel went over to the bar and placed his order; he made towards a table adjacent to where the two men were sitting, and passing the time of day, Martin said to him, 'Colonel Briggs, this is Mr Muller.' Rolf rose from his seat and they shook hands.

'Would you care to join us, Colonel?' Rolf asked.

'Don't mind if I do; but I hope I'm not intruding.'

Having been assured that he was not intruding, the colonel sat down with the other two. 'Been taking my daily constitutional over the common,' he told them.

The Piltdown Golf Club is situated on common land, and because of this, access to the golf course is available to the public, and as the common affords ideal walking facilities, many people take advantage of this, with varying degrees of annoyance on both sides. Colonel Briggs had never played golf; the wild life on the common appealed to him much more than the sporting activities. Most of his neighbours in Maresfield Park were members at Piltdown, and one or two of them had attempted several times to persuade him to join; but he was not interested.

The colonel knew Martin Bell from his occasional attendance at the parish church, and although he himself was not a religious man, he nevertheless respected Martin for his beliefs. His wife was a more regular worshipper than he, and took an active part in the social side of church life.

The three men were served with their meal, and the serious business of eating occupied them for twenty minutes or so. The silence was broken by Colonel Briggs who, turning to Rolf said, 'You must be the young fellow the rector was telling me about. He came up to see Maude yesterday about the church garden fete, and was mentioning a young man he'd met who was interested in the old park. Well now, I happen to own quite a slice of it, and if you'd like to take a look round the place you're more than welcome.'

'Colonel Briggs, you are so kind, and I'd very much like to do so.'

'Tell you what I'll do,' said the colonel, 'I'll have a word with my wife, and I'll give you a call. You're staying at The Chequers I believe?'

The meal over, Rolf offered to drive the colonel back into Maresfield, but the old soldier preferred to resume his walk.

'Wouldn't do to get soft,' he said, and away he went across the road and, climbing a fence as a schoolboy might, he went striding across the field in the direction of a large wooded area with a beautiful lake, where no doubt he would pause for a while to admire the water lilies which grew there in abundance. On through Park Farm and, taking the path through the churchyard, he would in a very short time be back within the boundaries of Maresfield Park, and within a quarter of a mile of home.

As they drove towards Maresfield, Martin expressed his thanks to Rolf for the interest he had shown in his father.

'The old man doesn't get many visitors,' he said. 'It's easy to forget old folk shut away in homes. My wife is troubled badly with rheumatism, otherwise she would have him at home with us.' As they approached Martin's neat little cottage, the blacksmith said, 'Will you spare a few minutes to come in and see my wife. It'll mean a lot to her. Being unable to get about much, she sees very few people.'

'Of course,' replied Rolf, 'I'd be delighted.'

Despite her severe handicap, Rolf found Grace Bell to be a pleasant and happy person. She greeted her husband with a kiss, and warmly welcomed the young man into her home.

'What a pleasure it is to meet you, Mr Muller. I was hoping my husband wouldn't let you get away without calling on me. How kind of you to take him along to see his father.'

'It was a pleasure for me to do so, Mrs Bell, and also a privilege,' he replied. 'It is also a pleasure to make your acquaintance.'

The cottage was spotlessly clean, and furnished with hand-crafted items of oak; a corner cupboard, a sideboard, book shelves and several exquisite small tables. Rolf could not restrain himself from expressing his admiration of the quality of workmanship. Mrs Bell beamed with pleasure as Rolf examined them, and she took great pride in telling him that they had all been made by her father who had been a master joiner and cabinetmaker. She told him that as a young man, her father had assisted her grandfather in making several pieces of furniture for Prince Munster, and some of these items were still in the possession of one or two Maresfield families.

Rolf would have stayed longer had he not remembered that he was expected for tea at old Mrs Prewett's. It was three o'clock by the time he arrived back at The Chequers. There were two telephone messages for him; one was from the rector and the other was from Colonel Briggs. He rang the colonel, who having had a talk with his wife invited him to dine with them that evening; strictly informal, of course, and if he would care to come round about seven o'clock they could take a turn in the grounds while it was still daylight. Rolf was happy with the arrangement and was pleased to accept. The rector was apparently not at home when Rolf attempted to return his call; there was no reply.

Having freshened himself up, Rolf decided that he would walk to his appointment with old Mrs Prewett as no particular time had been set, and the exercise would be good for him. It was four o'clock when he tapped at the cottage door. The door was opened by an elegant lady who was so much like Kitty Glover that Rolf had no difficulty in recognising the relationship.

'Come in, Mr Muller,' the lady said, holding out her hand. 'I'm Connie Glover, Mrs Prewett's daughter.'

Shaking her hand, Rolf exclaimed, 'Yes, I can see; you are so very much like Kitty.'

Old Kitty Prewett sat in her chair looking with pleasurable anticipation towards the door. Her daughter had obviously spent some time preparing her for her visitor. Her silver hair had been neatly brushed, and she was wearing a beautiful new dress. Rolf walked over to shake hands with her, but instead of her hand she offered her cheek to be kissed. Rolf did not disappoint her. What a gallant young man; the very image of dear little Karl.

While Connie Glover busied herself with tea-time preparation Rolf sat close to old Mrs Prewett. Occasionally she would cause him slight embarrassment by leaning over towards him and murmuring.

'Such a sweet little boy,' whilst stroking him gently on the cheek and running her fingers through his hair. From time to time, prompted by her daughter, she would compose herself and resume a normal conversation. Rolf told her of his visit to old Mr Bell at Rockwood, and she told him that she had known both him and his father all her life. She began recalling days as a young girl, when she and her friends on their way to and from school, would look in at the door of the smithy and chat with the blacksmith. She talked of an age when children could walk freely in woods and meadows gathering blackberries and wild flowers, of outdoor picnics, of boys looking for birds' nests; all in complete safety.

Although Kitty had lived the whole of her long life without the advantage of money, she had always enjoyed the riches of a happy family life. She had been born into an environment where there had been love, and she had always believed in a loving God. She had something with which no amount of preaching or advanced theological persuasion could compare; what it was could clearly be seen in the face of this dear old lady.

Rolf noticed that the table had been laid with five places, and he wondered why; he did not have to speculate for long. Kitty Glover came through the door looking quite refreshing in a pretty white summer dress, and Rolf's heart took a sudden leap when he saw that she was followed by Daphne Charnford, looking to his mind, even more beautiful, though in a different way, than her friend. Both the young ladies made straight towards Granny Prewett to give her the kisses she anticipated. Kitty remained to talk with her, and Daphne greeted Mrs Glover with a warmth that was clearly reciprocated as they also began to talk together.

Rolf had risen from his seat as the girls entered, and Kitty smiled and said a demure hello. He had been on his feet for five minutes or more before Daphne turned from her conversation with Connie Glover and, apparently noticing him for the first time, she rewarded him with a smile so bewitching that it rendered an apology superfluous.

'Good afternoon, Rolf,' she said, 'I hope you don't mind our dropping in on your teaparty.'

'. . . er, no, Daphne,' he stammered. He was confused and could hardly trust himself to speak in case he might say something foolish. Noticing his discomfort, Daphne said, 'Do let's sit down. Kitty's taken Granny over for the next two hours. Tell me what you've been doing with yourself today.'

He told her of his visit to Rockwood with Martin Bell, about lunch at The Peacock, and his meeting with Colonel Briggs; how Martin had taken him to meet his wife, and the very pleasant half hour he'd spent in her company.

'She is such a charming and interesting lady. How sad it is that she is so severely crippled; I am truly amazed at her cheerfulness.'

'Mummy drops in to see her whenever she can,' said Daphne, 'but I don't know how long it is since she was last there. I must confess I haven't seen her for years, and yet I owe such a lot to her; she taught Kitty and me in Sunday School. I'll ask Kitty if she'll come with me to pay her a visit.'

'I'm sure that will give her much pleasure,' said Rolf.

Changing the subject, Daphne suddenly asked, 'What do you think of Colonel Briggs? I hope he didn't put you off with his bark.'

'His bark? I don't understand.'

'His loud voice. He sometimes forgets he's no longer on the parade ground. Apart from that, he's really quite a poppet.'

'Oh, I see,' said Rolf. 'He was extremely friendly, and would you believe it, he asked me to go round this evening to have dinner with him.'

'My, my,' Daphne chuckled, 'and you less than a week in England.'

'I think,' said Rolf, 'the real reason for the invitation is so that he can show me his gardens. It will be a wonderful opportunity for me to see a part of the old Maresfield Park estate.'

Mrs Glover announced that tea was ready and asked them all to take their places. Rolf was seated next to Granny Prewett, and Connie, her daughter, sat at her left hand in order to attend to her requirements. Daphne and Kitty busied themselves pouring tea and passing sandwiches. They were secretly amused by the formality of the occasion, but in honour of her German guest old Kitty had insisted that everything should be done correctly. Conversation at the table was kept to a minimum, and Rolf limited himself to a few complimentary remarks which caused the old lady to beam with pleasure.

After tea, Rolf thanked all the ladies for a most pleasant afternoon. He would have liked to have stayed longer, but mindful of his evening commitment, he begged to be excused. As he prepared to leave, Kitty Glover held up her hand in horror and said, 'Oh dear, I almost forgot; I have something for you, Rolf. Daddy had this sent up by special messenger.' She took from her bag a large envelope which she handed over to him. 'I'm so sorry, Rolf.'

'That's all right, Kitty.' He opened it up with mingled surprise and curiosity, and he first extracted a short memo which had been hastily scribbled. It read, 'Heard you were interested in the old Maresfield Park estate. Hope the enclosed may be of some interest. Raymond Glover.'

There were photostat copies of plans dated 1927, and a further large plan of the Maresfield Park Estate as it existed until then; also a few faded old photographs of various parts of the estate. Also enclosed were drawings showing future planned development.

Rolf was overcome by the generosity of a man he had not even met. He could not find the words he wanted to say, but the ladies were aware of his deep appreciation.

Turning to Daphne, Kitty said, 'I'll help Mummy with the washing up.'

Rolf seized the opportunity to ask Daphne if he might walk with her as they were both going in roughly the same direction. Daphne protested mildly to Kitty that she ought to lend a hand, but her friend insisted that her help was not required, and Rolf was rewarded with the acceptance of his offer.

As they walked towards the centre of the village, Mrs Croft, the postman's wife was coming out of the grocer's shop. Seeing the two young people walking towards her, she went back inside.

'Have you forgotten something?' queried the grocer.

'No, Mr Turley, but see who's about to pass the door. I reckon it's that German chap, and he's got Daphne Charnford with him.' George Turley would dearly have loved to have gone outside, and have just by chance, happened to encounter the two young people; but it was not to be. He could never let it be said of him that he ever went out of his way to interest himself in the affairs of other people. Instead, he contented himself with observing to Mrs Croft,

'Oh yes, I saw them earlier on as they walked down the road.'

They walked as far as the Charnford drive entrance when Daphne said, 'Thank you for walking me home, Rolf. I mustn't take up any more of your time if you're going out again this evening. Do let me know how you get on with the colonel.'

Rolf, realising that time was getting short, and that he still had a lot of things to do, reluctantly said goodbye to her, but he stood and watched as she went gracefully along the drive until she came to a bend in the roadway. He was rewarded with a wave of her hand as she turned, before disappearing out of sight.

When Rolf arrived at The Chequers, the first thing he did was to telephone the rector. When he was connected with the reverend gentleman he made his apologies for the delay in returning his call.

'Don't apologise, Mr Muller,' the rector said. 'I've been away from home most of the afternoon. What I wondered was this. We are having our annual church garden fete on Saturday, the twenty-seventh, and if you are still here on that day, will you be willing to perform the opening ceremony?'

Rolf was taken aback. He took some time to reply:

'Are you quite sure, sir, that this is something for me?'

'Well,' confessed the rector, 'your connection with Prince Munster makes you a very strong candidate for the job. The people of Maresfield will be attracted to the fete if you are there. Now I don't expect you to let me have your decision immediately, but if you could let me know by tomorrow afternoon I'd be very grateful. We have a parochial church council meeting in the evening.' Rolf expressed his thanks to the rector for the honour, and promised to give the matter his careful consideration.

Before preparing for his evening appointment, Rolf again opened the envelope Mr Glover had sent, and studied the documents. The plan of the original Maresfield Park Estate provided evidence of the size of the mansion, with its outhouses and stables, vast areas of lawn, gardens, pasturage and woodlands. There were many workmen's cottages, and one or two more substantial houses. There were also plans for the initial stages of development. Each proposed plot had its own set of plans and was given a number, and bore the name of the purchaser. Where trees were to be retained, these were shown on the plans. On some plots there were substantial numbers; on others merely oddments, and many showed none at all. It was apparent that a vast amount of tree felling had taken place.

Carefully putting away the documents, Rolf washed, shaved and dressed for the evening. He whistled happily, and felt that today was turning out fine.

9

Colonel Briggs and his wife were standing on the lawn when Rolf arrived at The Limes at exactly seven o'clock. The colonel hailed him as he came in sight with a cheery,

'Hello my dear chap. Good to see you; always appreciate punctuality. Meet my wife. Maude, this is the young man, Mr Muller.'

'I'm delighted to meet you, Mrs Briggs,' said Rolf holding out his hand, which the lady took and held a while.

'How do you do?' she responded formally, but with a smile of welcome. 'Charles says you are interested in The Park; it will be a pleasure for us both to show you a part of it. Now I hope you don't mind, but we shall be having just a very light meal, and I've taken the liberty of asking one or two neighbours to come round afterwards. I thought it would be a good idea for you to meet them.'

'You are both very kind,' said Rolf. 'I do appreciate what you are doing for me.'

Mrs Briggs asked to be excused as there were things to be done inside the house. The colonel suggested to Rolf that they should take a walk while it was still daylight.

'Maude is the expert. She'll catch up with us no doubt, just as soon as she's finished giving Mrs Jones a few last minute instructions.'

As they skirted the east side of the house, Rolf could see the reason why the property had been called The Limes. There was a row of a dozen or so lime trees bordering a paddock in which a couple of hunters were peacefully grazing. The scent of the limes was pleasing to the senses, and brought a comment from Rolf.

'There is something refreshing about the linden tree.'

'The linden tree? Oh the limes,' said the colonel, 'yes,

they are part of an avenue of limes that at one time stretched for more than a mile.'

They stood for a while looking at the two horses; one of them, whinnying with pleasure, came trotting across to the fence to be affectionately patted by his master. While they were standing there, Maude Briggs came out of the house, went over to the two men, and, at the sight of her, the other horse came over to join the party.

They left the paddock and made towards a small lake where a variety of ducks and geese swam lazily, and called out for tit-bits of food which Mrs Briggs had thoughtfully brought along with her. A small rowing boat moored on the far side of the lake bore witness to the fact that children were frequent visitors to the Briggs' estate. There were willow trees and alders dotted here and there around the lake's perimeter, and some of these were reflected in the still water.

Going a little further, they came to an area of trees, about twenty in all, mostly birch with a blue cedar in the middle. No oaks were to be seen, and Rolf felt a slight sense of disappointment. As they were approaching the cedar he looked down on the ground, and was somewhat surprised to see an acorn lying there. He stooped and picked it up, remarking to his companions,

'How strange that there should be an acorn here; I don't see oaks.'

The colonel laughed and said, 'It must have been dropped by a bird.'

Walking out of the wooded area they came to the boundary fence and, taking Rolf by the arm, Colonel Briggs pointed out to him the tops of some trees on the other side. How many trees there were Rolf could not tell, but they rose to a great height, and their foliage was quite dense; they were undoubtedly oaks.

'May I ask if this particular neighbour will be coming this evening?' Rolf enquired. The colonel's face turned a vivid scarlet; his moustache turned a somersault. His answer was short and to the point.

'No. He will not!'

Before Rolf had time to sink into the ground, Maude Briggs came to his rescue.

'Don't be upset, Mr Muller. You may have gathered that Charles and he are not the best of friends.'

'Friends, did you say? He's no friend of mine! Shouldn't think the bounder has any friends. Naval chap, don't you know.'

One or two more expletives and the colonel ran out of steam, leaving his wife to fill in the details of the feud.

'Commander Brewster has been having trouble on his property. It started five or six weeks ago; someone has been going in at night and digging holes in the ground. Why they should want to do such a thing is a complete mystery. The silly man came round and accused Charles of being responsible; said he must be jealous of his gardens or something equally foolish. It appears that on one occasion he surprised a couple of men with spades, and says they disappeared in this direction.'

Rolf felt distinctly uneasy and could find nothing to say. Mrs Briggs went on,

'The Brewsters have a most precocious child staying with them from time to time; their daughter's boy; name of Horace. Three weeks ago, Parkes our gardener caught him over at the lake side trying to get into the rowing boat. How he came to be there, goodness knows, but he was very rude and Parkes cuffed him about the ears and sent him off screaming. Charles saw the incident, but was too far away to do anything. Poor Parkes was rather worried that Charles might fire him, but we heard nothing from the Brewsters and so we're regarding the incident as closed.'

By the time they had arrived back at the house Colonel Briggs had regained his composure, and they were very soon enjoying the food skilfully prepared by Mrs Jones. The gazpacho was just the thing for a hot summer evening; it was most refreshing, and an excellent introduction to the buffet meal, complimented by a choice Chablis.

The first of the neighbours to arrive were Mr and Mrs Appleby. Gordon and Myrtle Appleby had spent most of their married life as tea planters in Ceylon (they could not bring themselves to refer to it as Sri Lanka). The Frobishers and the Colbeys arrived together, completing the party.

Mrs Frobisher was a member of the parochial church council, as was also Mrs Briggs, and those two ladies were soon in conversation concerning the coming church fete. Mrs Colbey and Mrs Appleby engaged themselves in talk of domestic matters. Colonel Briggs handed glasses of wine to the ladies before addressing himself to the men's requirements.

When he had finished the task of charging the glasses, the colonel said, 'Maude has been telling our young friend about the skirmish with Brewster and his confounded holes.'

'Yes,' said Peter Frobisher, 'he's a most unpleasant character; but I must say it's rather thick when you think about it; chaps going around digging holes on another chap's property.'

'Did you hear about George Barker's experience the other week?' put in Colonel Briggs. 'A fellow from Crawley came and asked if he could use a metal detector over his ground. Had some cock and bull story about doing a geological survey. Barker sent him off with a flea in his ear, but I heard there were a couple of others on the same game.'

Gordon Appleby joined in. 'I heard a conversation in The Chequers some two or three months ago. A fellow was buying drinks for a group of the local chaps and asking all sorts of questions about houses in The Park; for some reason or other he seemed particularly keen on oak trees.' He turned to Roger Colbey and observed,

'You've some fine oak trees, old chap; it's a wonder the blighters haven't pestered you.'

Colbey looked somewhat sheepishly at the others and said, 'I wasn't going to mention it; I feel such a fool, but one of them did call while I was away from home, and Beryl fell for it. She let the fellow loose about the place and he spent a couple of hours rooting about among the trees; kept away from the rest of the grounds. I've been keeping a close watch ever since, but nothing more seems to have happened.'

Colonel Briggs enlightened the others by saying, 'Herr Muller and I lunched together at The Peacock. He was entertaining a fellow from the village; Bell, the old blacksmith. Bell introduced us, and he kindly asked me to join them; very civil I thought. Heard from the padre that the young man was interested in The Park, so when I got home I suggested to Maude that we might ask him round to meet one or two of the residents.'

'How do you come to have an interest in The Park, Mr Muller?' asked Gordon Appleby, and then jocularly, 'You're not a geologist, are you?'

'No,' Rolf laughed and said, 'I assure you I don't go around with a spade. Perhaps I should explain. My grandfather often came to Maresfield Park as a child, and he told me so many wonderful things about his holidays here. His father and Prince Munster were distant relatives and also very close friends. Before my grandfather died I made him a promise that I would pay a visit to see the old home. The possibility of development had not occurred to him, and my family allowed him to live in peace with his memories. We ourselves expected that there would be many changes, but I was surprised to find it so entirely different from what I had always imagined it would be like.'

'Time doesn't stand still,' said Peter Frobisher, 'but when you compare it with many other developments in the south of the country, we haven't done such a bad job in maintaining the peace and tranquillity of the countryside. We have a first class residents' association here in The Park, and it does a fine job in keeping out the undesirables.'

Although Rolf was himself heir to a long line of nobility, he could not help feeling a sense of discomfort at what he recognised as a somewhat snobbish attitude from someone he suspected of being a recently arrived member of his present station. Rolf's own breeding would not permit him to voice the slightly contentious thoughts that came into his mind, and he contented himself with a quizzical furrowing of the brow.

Roger Colbey was of a different mould. He was a man in his seventies who had held a position of responsibility in the diplomatic service which, in normal circumstances, would have led to a peerage; but such honour was not to be his. His untimely departure from public life had been occasioned by his propensity for subordinating diplomacy to integrity, and while he was denied the honour of investiture, he retained his dignity. He had put his years of retirement to good use and had gained for himself a considerable reputation as a local historian. This meeting with the young man was particularly fortunate, as he was experiencing some difficulty in verifying certain facts concerning the Munster family.

Seeing in the young man a potential source of invaluable first-hand information, Roger asked him if he would be willing to give him some assistance in his research. Rolf was happy to find himself in a situation of being able to return some of the kindness he had been shown since coming to Maresfield, and he readily agreed to co-operate. It was arranged that he should pay a visit to Colbridge on the Friday morning and have coffee with Roger and Beryl Colbey.

The two men returned to the small group which had gathered together, the wives having joined their menfolk. The ladies were soon captivated by the courteousness of the handsome young German, and the men looked on with amusement as they vied with each other for his attention. In a tone very much resembling that of her husband, Doris Frobisher took over the conversation. 'Do tell us; where exactly in Germany is your home, Mr Muller?'

'Langentopf,' said Rolf. 'It is a small provincial town with a population of twenty thousand, and is on the banks of the River Elbe not far from the city of Hamburg.'

'And what is your profession, or should I say trade?' she persisted.

'I have until now neither profession nor trade' Rolf replied, 'but I have studied medicine in Heidelberg. My father is director of the Lintzen Clinic, and I hope to join him there at the beginning of next year.'

Sensing that matters were becoming a little strained, Maude Briggs observed gently. 'We're not going to ask you for your curriculum vitae, Mr Muller,' and, turning to the rest of the party, 'Now, who would like coffee?'

'Not for us, thank you, we'd better be going,' said Mrs

Frobisher. 'Peter has a busy day ahead of him tomorrow.'
She looked at her husband as if defying him to contradict
her, and in the interests of marital harmony, he wisely
concurred.

After their neighbours had all gone home, Maude
Briggs said, 'I trust you are not too exhausted, Mr Muller.
It is always a problem to know who to invite on occasions
like this, and I'm afraid dear Mrs Frobisher can be rather
tiresome sometimes. They are fairly new to the
neighbourhood, but I fear they seem to be doing their
best to take over. However, don't you think the Colbeys
are charming people?'

Rolf ignored the remarks about the Frobishers, but
hastened to agree about the Colbeys. The colonel insisted
that they all had a nightcap, after which Rolf prepared to
leave.

'Thank you so much for a wonderful evening. It is an
experience I shall never forget. I am overwhelmed by the
friendly reception I have had in Maresfield.'

'May we have the pleasure of seeing you again before
you return to Germany, Mr Muller?' Mrs Briggs asked.

'I would not think of leaving without calling on you
again,' Rolf replied, 'but I'm not sure when it will be.'

10

Having left The Limes, Rolf began a leisurely walk towards the village. He went over again in his mind the things he had heard during the evening. He strongly felt the need to confide in someone. It was too late in the day to do anything about it immediately, but he determined that in the morning, he would contact Chris Charnford.

As he mused on the events of the day, his thoughts were interrupted by a piercing scream coming from the direction of the parish church. Could he possibly have imagined it? He quickened his pace until he arrived at the churchyard where he stood, listening intently, peering into the darkness. There was not a thing to be seen but the gaunt outlines of gravestones. He was about to cross the road towards The Chequers when there was a muffled sound, followed by the breaking of a twig.

Having no regard for his own safety, he rushed towards the direction of the sound, and then he saw the figure of a girl being dragged by two men in the church car park, towards a grey car with its engine running. The girl was putting up a brave struggle and, encouraged by the arrival of assistance, she made a desperate lunge at one of her assailants while his companion was occupied in opening the rear door of the car. The next moment, the thug who was struggling to hold the girl was knocked to the ground, by a stunning blow. As he lay groaning on the ground, the other brute leapt at Rolf, aiming blows at his head.

The girl seemed to want to stay and help her rescuer, but he called to her to run for it; even so, she hung around long enough to ensure that he had gained the upper hand. Before leaving the car park Rolf was careful to note the registration number of the vehicle, and as the villains picked themselves up from the ground they poured out a string of invective, only half of which was understood by the German. No further time was lost by the pair of cowards; the car was soon speeding along the Haywards Heath road.

The church clock was striking the hour of midnight as Rolf entered The Chequers. The girl had gone ahead of him and was being comforted by Pat Broxon while her husband spoke on the telephone. Charles Broxon was aghast when he saw Rolf come in looking dishevelled, and his conversation came to a sudden stop.

Addressing Rolf he gasped,

'Rolf! not you Rolf; oh no, not you?'

Rolf could not think what Charles was talking about, but realising that he was probably speaking to the police, he called out the car's registration number while it was still fresh in his mind, and Charles repeated it into the telephone before absentmindedly replacing the receiver.

'How could you?' Charles said to Rolf. 'You filthy beast.'

Rolf wasn't ready for this. Ignoring Charles' outburst he went over to where the girl was sitting and was amazed to see that it was Nancy, the barmaid.

'Mr Muller,' she gasped, 'it was you. Oh thank you, thank you.'

Realizing his dreadful mistake, Charles Broxon looked at Rolf and said to him,

'Rolf, I'm so sorry; I didn't know. What a fool I am.'

Rolf forced a grin and replied, 'Don't worry, Charles; I only hope the ruffians will be caught. They went in the direction of Haywards Heath .'

'I'll get on to the police again,' Charles said, and he lost no time in contacting the police station in Uckfield.

'Yes,' they said, 'we assumed that what you gave us over the telephone was the number of the getaway car, and we've put out a call for a block on all roads leading out of Maresfield. We've also sent an officer and a woman constable to interview the young lady. They should be with you in a very short time.'

'They'll also be able to interview the gentleman who saved her,' said Charles, 'he's here with us.'

Within five minutes the landlord was opening the door

to admit PC Thompson and WPC Small. Ascertaining that Nancy had sufficiently recovered from her state of shock, WPC Small took her aside and requested a statement from her, while PC Thompson was similarly engaged with Charles and Rolf.

The bar had been particularly busy, as The Chequers had been hosting a darts match. The visiting team from Hartfield had brought their supporters along with them and the inn had been crowded most of the evening. Along with her brother Percy, Nancy had been rushed off her feet, and had little time to respond to the good-natured banter from the customers. Charles had kept a watching brief from the end of the bar counter. Apart from the regular customers, he was able to recognise most of the visitors from Hartfield. They were a friendly crowd.

There were, so far as Charles could ascertain, only four or five complete strangers. Of these, he noticed one in particular eyeing Nancy in an unwholesome way. This man would, from time to time, nudge his companion, and the pair of them would leer in her direction. Fortunately, Nancy was too engrossed in her work to notice, but the protective Charles decided to keep them under close observation. This was by no means the first time that Nancy had been ogled; after all, she was an extremely attractive young lady. Apart from being a responsible employer, Charles also had the interests of his son, Nancy's fiancé, at heart.

The constable asked for a description of the two men, and this Charles was able to supply with accuracy, even down to the tattoo on the wrist of one of them. Both of them, he estimated, would be in their late twenties; they wore blousons; one blue, the other grey, with open necked shirts and light coloured slacks; and both wore training shoes.

'Is it usual for the young lady to walk home alone?' the constable asked.

'No it isn't,' replied Charles, 'she just lives a couple of hundred yards along the road, and I usually watch her until she reaches her gate. Tonight she wanted particularly to be home early, and I hadn't finished checking the tills when she left. I thought her brother

Percy would have seen her home; he's been working here this evening.'

'And now, sir,' said the constable to Rolf, 'where do you fit in?'

Rolf gave the officer details of the circumstances which had led up to his involvement in the incident. He could not give an accurate description of the men; being involved in the act of rescue, he had had no time to study their mode of dress, but he agreed that they could feasibly have been the pair described by Charles Broxon. He described the car; a grey Ford Cortina and repeated its registration number.

The telephone rang; it was the Uckfield Police Station. The wanted car had been stopped at a road block between Scaynes Hill and Newick; the two occupants had been brought in for questioning, and it was requested that Charles and Rolf might go along with the two police officers to see if they could identify the men. Rolf would very much have preferred going to bed, but he was anxious to help in any way he could, and so he made no objection.

Arriving at the police station, Charles and Rolf were ushered into the charge room where the station officer, Sergeant Graham, along with two constables, stood facing two young men looking battered and belligerent.

'Thank you for coming, gentlemen,' the sergeant said. 'These two men are assisting us in our inquiries into an incident at Maresfield involving a young lady believed to be employed by you, sir. No charges have yet been made, but could you please tell me if either or both of them are known to you.'

'No, I don't know either of them,' said Charles, 'but they were both in The Chequers all the evening.'

Both men glared malevolently at the innkeeper, and one of them cried out, 'That's a lie. We've not been anywhere near the place.'

'No doubt you can produce witnesses to their having been there?' queried the sergeant.

'Without any trouble, sergeant,' said Charles.

'And you, sir?' said the sergeant, addressing Rolf.

'I'm sure these are the ones I fought with,' was his

reply.

'Thank you,' said the sergeant, and he accompanied the two gentlemen out of the room, leaving the constable with the miserable pair.

Outside the room Sergeant Graham said, 'They'll be charged and locked up here overnight. Tomorrow they will be appearing before a magistrate at a special hearing. Will you make arrangements to be here please, at eleven o'clock? We shall send a patrol car for the young lady; it should all be over in about ten minutes. The usual form is for them to be remanded in custody at Lewes prison for trial at the Crown Court.'

To Rolf he said, 'You were very brave to tackle those two, sir; I wish there were more about like you. We've suspected them for several jobs over a long period, but we've never been able to nail them down.'

It was almost three o'clock when Rolf finally got to bed. He had always been a sound sleeper, and he was soon in a state of oblivion. It seemed that his head had only just touched the pillow when he was awakened by a loud knocking on his bedroom door. It was Charles Broxon; 'Are you awake Rolf? It's a quarter past nine and we've to be in Uckfield by eleven.'

Rolf forced himself into wakefulness and said he'd be down shortly, it took him just twenty minutes to wash, shave and dress himself. Breakfast was awaiting him when he arrived down below, and Charles joined him at the table.

'I've been along to see Nancy,' he said. 'She's none the worse for her experience, but I've told her she must see the doctor before she comes back to work. She's as tough as nails; I'm sure that if there'd been only one of those blighters she'd have given a good account of herself. She was singing your praises old chap. You're a knight in shining armour as far as she's concerned.'

Brushing aside the flattery, Rolf said, 'I've a few important telephone calls to make before I go into Uckfield.'

He finished breakfast in record time and returned to his room, emerging a few moments later with his pocket diary in his hand. Down in the reception lobby he picked up the telephone and dialled the number of the Charnford household. The call was answered by Mrs Charnford. Rolf wished her a pleasant good morning and asked to speak to Chris.

'I'm sorry, Rolf, he's already out riding on the forest. Can I give him a message?'

'Would you tell him that I'd like to have a talk with him please? It's quite important,' Rolf said. 'I'm going out for a time this morning, but I'll wait in at The Chequers this afternoon.' 'Well now, why don't you come and have lunch with us, Rolf? We'd be very pleased to have you,' Mrs Charnford said.

'Why thank you; I'd be very happy to do so,' he replied.

'One o'clock then, or come whenever you're ready. Goodbye, Rolf.'

The Reverend Percival Truscott was preparing for a morning in the garden when the telephone rang.

'Oh good morning, Mr Muller; I hope you have some good news for me.'

'I shall be very happy to open your garden fete, sir,' Rolf told him.

'Splendid, splendid! My committee will be so pleased. As you know, we're meeting this evening to finalise details; I'll be in touch with you again soon.' He would have continued talking at length, but Rolf asked to be excused as he anticipated having a busy morning.

As the station sergeant had predicted, the special hearing was over in little over ten minutes. The two miscreants, Ritchie and Robertson, were committed to the remand wing at Lewes prison to await trial at Crown Court. Nancy joined Charles and Rolf as they emerged into the street; she grabbed hold of Rolf's hand, shaking it vigorously. Before Rolf could ask how she was feeling she said, 'How can I ever thank you, Mr Muller? I do hope you were not badly hurt.'

'It was a great pleasure to help you, Nancy. No, as you can see, I am not hurt.'

'You do realise, don't you,' Charles observed to Rolf, 'that you'll have to come back to give evidence at the trial?'

'Oh my goodness,' moaned Rolf. 'When is that likely to be?'

At that moment Charles noticed Sergeant Graham coming towards them.

'Oh, sergeant, can we trouble you for a moment? When is the trial likely to be?'

'I'm afraid I can't tell you that, sir. The next Crown Court is on September 22nd, but there's no chance of it being heard then. Depends on how many they've got on the waiting list; could be months.'

'Does that mean that I shall have to come back to England specially?' asked Rolf.

'Afraid so,' replied the sergeant. 'Couldn't have the trial without you, sir; you're a key witness. Don't worry though, they'll give you plenty of notice.'

11

Rolf arrived at the livery stables just as Chris was unsaddling. One of the hands came over and took charge of the horses, leaving Chris free to talk to his new friend.

'Hello, Rolf, this is an unexpected pleasure. Won't you come inside?'

'Of course,' said Rolf. 'I've been invited to lunch.'

'Good old Daphne,' chuckled Chris.

'Your mother invited me,' continued Rolf. 'I rang this morning, but I missed you. I asked your mother if she would give you a message, and she kindly suggested that I might come and lunch with you.'

Chris realised his mistake in jumping to the conclusion that it was his sister who had given the invitation; he could have bitten his tongue. However, Rolf had not reacted to the Freudian slip, and may therefore not have noticed it.

They walked together into the house and Sylvia Charnford welcomed them. She said to Chris, 'I'll talk to Rolf while you go and change your clothes, and then I'll leave you to talk together. Lunch will be ready in half an hour. Daphne is visiting Mrs Bell, and Father's gone into the village to post some letters.'

Chris excused himself and went up to his room, returning after twenty minutes to find his mother and Rolf engrossed in earnest conversation.

'Daphne was saying, Rolf, that you had pricked her conscience when you told her you had been to see Grace Bell. I too must try to find time to call on her; I'm afraid I've neglected her rather badly. The trouble is that we're having a church garden fete at the end of next week, and it has taken up so much of my time. We have a meeting this evening to finalise the arrangements. It still hasn't been decided who will open it; Lady Grantwell was asked three months ago if she would perform the opening ceremony. At first she accepted; then she changed her mind as Sir Harold was planning a cruise. Five weeks ago she informed the rector that she might well open it after all, but would let him have her decision by Friday of last week. On Tuesday of this week, the rector was becoming desperate and tried to telephone Lady Grantwell, but was told she was away for a few days.'

Chris joined in, 'The rector will have to put his skates on and get someone else.'

Rolf felt a little uncomfortable as he said, 'He already has. He's asked me to do it.'

There was a long pause, and then Mrs Charnford broke the silence. 'That's an excellent idea - revolutionary, but excellent. Perhaps I'm not supposed to know about it until the rector puts it to the meeting, but I do hope you will accept, Rolf.'

Rolf smiled and said, 'You are so wise, Mrs Charnford.'

Sylvia departed in the direction of the kitchen, leaving the two young men to discuss the matter on Rolf's mind.

'Chris,' he began, 'there is something I need to talk over with you. May I take you into my confidence?'

'You may, Rolf, if you are quite sure that is what you want to do,' Chris replied. Having been assured that Rolf had considered the matter carefully, Chris listened attentively as his friend began to reveal the true reason for his coming to Maresfield. The events of yesterday evening at The Limes had brought him to the realisation that on his own, he had no chance of uncovering the secret of The Park. From the conversation there it had become clear that people other than himself were interested in what had lain buried on the estate for nearly seventy years.

Rolf told Chris of the deathbed promise he had made to his grandfather. He produced the faded old diary and showed Chris the entry for the month of August 1914 - MARESFIELD PARK - FIVE OAKS - THREE PACES RIGHT. He gave him the full story of how his grandfather, as a child of nine, had witnessed the strange procession in Maresfield Park, and the burying of the chest.

'I visited Colonel Briggs yesterday evening,' said Rolf, 'and I met three other gentlemen and their wives. There were Mr and Mrs Frobisher, Mr and Mrs Appleby and Mr and Mrs Colbey. They were discussing mysterious happenings in The Park; of people searching the ground with metal detectors, and of holes being dug on certain properties. All these events lead me to suspect that I am not the only person who has heard about the secret of Maresfield Park.'

Chris paused for some time to absorb the significance of the things Rolf had told him. Eventually he said, 'Thank you for taking me into your confidence, Rolf. Let's leave it for now, and give me time to do some quiet thinking.'

Mrs Charnford called them to lunch, and when they came into the dining-room, Daphne was already sitting at the table. She rose as they entered, and Rolf walked over to shake the proffered hand.

'Hello, Rolf. How nice to see you,' she said.

'Good afternoon,' he replied, 'It is a pleasure to see you again.'

While they were standing, Arthur Charnford came into the room with his wife. He made directly towards Rolf and gripped his hand.

'Well done, well done,' he exclaimed fervently, 'I'm proud to know you.' Rolf, taken by surprise, made no response.

'What's all this about, Daddy?' asked Daphne.

'Yes, come on, Dad,' Chris joined in, 'What do you know that we don't?'

When Rolf had sufficiently recovered he murmured, 'Oh, thank you, sir, but it was nothing.'

'Nothing?' Arthur said. 'I suppose you rescue damsels in distress every day of your life. The village is buzzing with excitement this morning, and Charles Broxon's doing a roaring lot of trade at The Chequers. But hasn't Rolf told you?'

Three voices raised as one said, 'Told us what?'

'Well now,' Arthur continued, 'I've heard three completely different versions, but each one makes Rolf a hero. Let's hear what you have to say, Rolf.'

Rolf had no wish to be called a hero, and he felt decidedly uncomfortable, but neither did he wish to appear churlish, and so he proceeded to give a potted version of what had happened.

'I was walking back to The Chequers when I heard a scream. I located the source of the trouble, and I saw two men attacking a young lady who I later discovered was Nancy, the barmaid at The Chequers Inn. I was able to assist her to escape from them and I had the satisfaction of knocking one of them to the ground; I believe the other may have had some damage done to his jaw. Their intention seems to have been to drag Nancy into their car, as the engine was running, but they seem to have changed their minds and made off rather hurriedly.' And that, as far as Rolf was concerned, was all there was to tell.

Sylvia called them to their seats and lunch was served. This was Rolf's first encounter with farmhouse food in England, and in order to allow him to savour it to the full, conversation was kept to a minimum. Chris, however, asked his father, 'Were they local men?'

'Someone called Ritchie; Mike Ritchie I believe, and the other a Jack Robertson,' said his father. 'They are both from Crawley; apparently they're well-known to the police over a wide area.' Daphne could not restrain herself from giving Rolf an admiring glance, and softly she said, 'I hope you weren't hurt, Rolf.'

He gave her a reassuring smile which brought a blush to her cheek, and she felt a disconcerting flutter within her which made her realise that she could no longer pretend to herself that this man could never be more than an interesting stranger.

When lunch was over, the three men withdrew to the garden. Chris asked to be excused for a few minutes as he had some urgent business matters to discuss with his father. Taking a stroll across the lawn in the direction of the summer house, Rolf was fascinated by the variety of flowers growing in the herbaceous border; there were some he had never seen before. He stood admiring a cluster of campanula, growing to almost four feet in height, with beautiful blue bellflowers. As he gazed in silence he heard a gentle cough, and as he turned he saw

Daphne coming towards him bearing a tray with a pot of coffee and two cups. She asked Rolf to get chairs from the summerhouse, and she selected a place for them to sit.

'Did Mummy tell you, I've been to see Mrs Bell this morning?' she asked.

'Yes,' Rolf said. 'How is she?'

'She seemed quite bright, considering the amount of pain she must be suffering. Mr Bell says your visit bucked her up no end.'

'I've been thinking quite a lot since I met Mrs Bell,' Rolf said.

'Surely, there is something that can be done.'

'She's been waiting for several months to go into hospital for an operation,' Daphne said, 'but there's a very long waiting list. If she had the money she could have it done privately, but the cost would be far more than they can afford.'

Rolf remained silent for several minutes; an idea was forming in his mind. Eventually he said, 'My father is a leading authority on rheumatology; he has a private clinic. perhaps he can be persuaded to take her. This evening I'll telephone him and ask what he can do.'

'Oh Rolf, it would be wonderful if something like that could be arranged,' Daphne exclaimed enthusiastically.

'We'd better not say anything about it until I've spoken to my father,' Rolf said cautiously, 'but I'm sure there will be something he can do. I'm due to join him at The Lintzen Clinic in January of next year, but I'll offer to start earlier.'

'How will she get over there?' queried Daphne.

'That will depend on when Father can fit her in. If it can be done quite soon, then I shall take her. I shall have to engage a nurse to accompany us, of course.'

'Will she need to be a qualified nurse?' Daphne wanted to know.

'Oh no,' answered Rolf. 'All that will be required of her is that she should be caring and conscientious.'

Daphne found herself saying, 'Would I qualify?'

Rolf couldn't believe what he heard, and certainly could not accept that she was being serious.

'You'd be perfect,' he said, not dreaming that the

question was asked in earnest.

'Good; then I should very much like to offer my services. What are my chances?'

'Excellent,' Rolf grinned. 'Have you ever been to Germany?'

'Not since I was a child,' Daphne replied, 'but I have regular correspondence with a German penfriend. Her home is in Iserlohn in Westphalia. Have you ever heard of it?'

'Yes,' said Rolf. 'I've actually been there. I have a friend from University who lives at Soest in Westphalia; it is about fifty kilometres from Iserlohn. It may be possible to visit, but we must wait and see what my father says before we start to make plans.'

Out of the corner of her eye, Daphne saw Chris approaching and quickly changed the subject.

'How did you get on with Colonel Briggs?' she asked.

'Very well indeed. Both he and Mrs Briggs were delightful hosts, and I also met a few other people from The Park.'

With a roguish grin, Chris broke in, 'He met the Applebys, the Frobishers and the Colbeys, and now my pet, Rolf and I have some serious talking to do; so if you'll excuse us ...'

Rolf began gallantly to protest, 'Daphne's quite welcome to stay as far as I'm concerned,' but Daphne cut him short.

'It's quite all right, Rolf. I must be getting back to give Mummy a hand in the kitchen.'

She gave him a conspiratorial smile and added, 'Let me know how you make out with your father.'

'You seem to have made quite a hit with Daphne,' Chris said. 'Do you think so?' Rolf asked. 'She's different from any other girl I know.'

'Now that you're a hero,' Chris teased, 'you'll have to get used to all the girls making a fuss of you.'

'Now Chris, please let's forget all that,' Rolf pleaded. 'Let's talk of other things.'

'It seems to me,' said Chris, 'we've got to keep our ears close to the ground. Who could possibly know about the chest without having heard about it from the people involved in the burying of it? It's going to be a lengthy process, but I would suggest a call on Martin Bell. Martin's father may recall the names of some of the men working on the estate at the time. If we can establish their names, we may be able to trace members of their families.'

Rolf was impressed by the idea, and suggested that they should make plans to visit the old man. Chris was thoughtful for a moment, then he said, 'Martin will be at the PCC meeting tonight; we'll ask Mother to give him a message. What do you say we spend the evening at The Chequers? We can have a bar snack about eight o'clock. I shouldn't think the meeting will last more than a couple of hours, so we'll ask Martin to call in on us on his way home.'

Before returning to The Chequers, Rolf called back in the house to thank Mrs Charnford for lunch; he also wanted to say goodbye to Daphne, but she wasn't there. Arthur Charnford walked out to the car with him, and he suggested that Rupert was due for some exercise if Rolf cared to take him out.

'I'll take him out on Friday afternoon if that's convenient,' Rolf said. 'Will three o'clock be a good time?'

'I'll see that he's ready for you,' Arthur replied.

12

Rolf returned to The Chequers and quietly went up to his room unseen by any of the staff. The first thing he did was to take out the plans and photographs that Raymond Glover had sent him. He took pencil and paper, and carefully made notes of any properties which were shown to have trees growing on them. He had no idea of the way he would go about the task of examining the actual wooded areas. He would certainly do nothing unlawful, and yet he could not take the risk of letting too many people in on his secret. So far only Chris was in on it, and Rolf doubted whether he would have the sort of influence necessary to obtain introduction to the exclusive circles in The Park.

At some stage or other he would have to take someone else into his confidence. He thought about Raymond Glover, and decided to seek Chris's thoughts on the matter. He liked what he had seen of Kitty's father, and the help he had already been given by him was very encouraging. In turn, he considered Colonel Briggs, the rector and Roger Colbey but on reflection, they were perhaps too old to be involved in anything so intriguing as this might subsequently prove to be.

Rolf began to feel drowsy, and so he put away the papers, and went over to his bed. He removed his shoes and put his feet up; his eyes closed and he was soon sleeping soundly. The sounds of traffic from the road below went unnoticed, and it was six o'clock before he eventually woke. He took a bath and dressed himself and he read a little before wandering down into the bar where the landlord and Nancy the barmaid were preparing for the evening trade.

'Hello, Rolf,' Charles called out. 'I didn't realise you

were here.'

'I've been having a lazy afternoon,' Rolf replied. 'I haven't felt so relaxed in years; the Maresfield air must be good for me.'

'The Press have been trying to contact you all afternoon. I don't think they believed me when I said I'd no idea where you were or when you'd be available. They're trying their best to get a story. They've been interviewing Nancy and they've taken photos of her; they particularly wanted a picture of the two of you together.'

Rolf was annoyed; he had no wish to be discourteous, but he said, 'If they're coming back, Charles, please let me know early enough so that I can arrange to be out.'

Charles was despondent; he was glad of the extra trade the events of the previous evening had brought, and Nancy had enjoyed the fuss she was receiving. But he had no wish to upset his guest and therefore he had to comply with Rolf's wishes.

'I'd like to make a phone call to Germany if that is convenient, Charles,' Rolf said. He had not noticed any public call boxes in the village, but as he would be conversing in German he was not unduly concerned at the possibility of being overheard.

'Of course, Rolf,' Charles said, 'go ahead; you know the drill.'

Rolf was amazed at the speed with which he was connected with his family; within half a minute he was talking to his mother. The first two minutes were spent in assuring her that he was all right; he had good accommodation, plenty of food and had made friends. Reluctantly Frau Muller handed the instrument to her husband; Rolf quickly dispensed with the courtesies and came to the point of his call.

'Father,' he said, 'I've come across a very advanced case of arthritis, and it seems that the lady is unable to receive the necessary treatment for many months. She is unable to afford private treatment here, and I hope you can help her. Is it possible for you to find a place for her at the clinic? Her husband has given me considerable assistance in my searches here and I should like to repay him for his kindness.'

Professor Muller took a few moments to reply, and then he said, 'You know we don't work miracles here, Rolf, but I will do what I can. As you know, it will be necessary to have the co-operation of her own doctor; you must get from him the lady's case history, and his written consent. There will be a vacant room on the third of September. How do you propose to get her here?'

'I shall drive her myself,' Rolf replied.

'Then you will need a nurse to accompany her,' his father said.

'That can easily be arranged; and Father, thank you.'

'You had better move quickly, my son, there is very little time to waste. If you miss the date I have given you, it will be the middle of next year before I can spare the time again. Now your sister wants to speak to you; I'll say goodbye.'

Rolf was very fond of his sister Helga. She was nineteen, and had her long golden hair in plaits hanging down her back. To her there was no-one like Rolf; he was her hero.

'Hello, Rolf; what are you getting up to, and when are you coming home?' she asked.

'I'm hoping to come on the third of September, and oh, I forgot to tell Mother I shall be bringing a young lady to stay with us, if that is convenient. Will you tell her for me, please?'

'Rolf!' Helga exclaimed, 'Don't tell me you have found a sweetheart.'

'No, nothing like that,' he assured her. 'I'm bringing a patient over to Father's clinic, and she will be travelling as nurse. Don't worry; you are still my favourite girl.'

They said their goodbyes and Rolf replaced the receiver. He then made a call to Daphne and told her,

'You can start packing your bags; Father has a vacancy from the third of September. I'm hoping to see Martin Bell this evening to put it to him; it is now up to him and Mrs Bell to accept.' 'You're an angel, Rolf,' she whispered.

Chris and Rolf met in The Chequers at eight o'clock. There were quite a number of customers already there, and as the two made their way to a table, heads began to turn in their direction. Rolf seemed not to notice, but Chris was aware of the attention they were attracting. He tried hard to ignore it, but it was difficult. There were many friendly nods, and people went out of their way to speak to them, but even this was irritating. There were lots of people unknown to Chris, and three men in particular glared malevolently in their direction.

While they were eating their meal, a man Rolf recognised as Peter Frobisher came into the bar. He had not seen the two friends, but he walked over to the three undesirables and sat at their table with his back towards Rolf and Chris. Frobisher engaged the three men in whispered but earnest conversation. When he had finished speaking, one of the three gave him a nudge, and with a raised eyebrow indicated that he should take a look over his shoulder. Frobisher looked slowly round and saw Chris and Rolf. Sheepishly he rose to his feet and walked over to their table.

'Why hello, Muller; hello Charnford,' he said jovially, 'I didn't see you as I came in. I'm just discussing a job I want these chaps to do for me; I'm thinking of having my drive relaid; I mustn't interrupt while you are eating, though.'

He returned to his table and talked rather more loudly on various trivialities before leaving the villainous trio.

13

The rector was not having things all his own way at the meeting of the parochial church council. The minutes of the previous meeting were read and duly approved. 'Matters arising' under normal circumstances would have passed without comment, but tonight there was the most important matter of the church fête. Mrs Frobisher reminded the rector that he was to contact Lady Grantwell and then report back concerning the opening ceremony. What had he to report? she wanted to know. The rector coughed nervously in order to clear his throat.

'As you all know,' he began, 'Lady Grantwell reconsidered her earlier decision, and said she might be prepared to open the fête after all; but we were told to wait for her final decision until Friday of last week.'

'Having had no word from her, I tried to telephone her, only to be told that she was out. By Tuesday of this week there was still no news of her; I therefore called at her home only to be told that she was unable to receive me. I'm sure you will agree that I had no alternative but to make other arrangements.'

'And have you made other arrangements?' demanded Mrs Frobisher.

'I have indeed,' replied the rector, with a smile.

'And with whom?' she wanted to know.

'We have staying in our village, a most distinguished young gentleman from Germany; he is related to the family of the late Prince Munster who was, as you all know, a greatly respected and loved landowner in this parish.'

There were nods of approval from half of the committee members, but others stared woodenly at the rector.

'Shouldn't we put it to the vote, Rector?' Mrs Frobisher asked, confident in her mind of the support of the majority of the committee.

'By all means, Mrs Frobisher, if you can suggest an alternative at such short notice.'

The lady was silent, and the rector asked, 'How many of you have met Mr Muller?'

The hands of Mr Bell, Mr Turley, Mrs Briggs, Mrs Charnford and Mrs Frobisher were raised.

'What is your impression of the young man, Mrs Briggs?' the rector asked.

'After a very brief acquaintance with him I found him to be a perfectly charming young gentleman, of impeccable breeding,' and, turning to Mrs Frobisher, she said, 'and you were absolutely enchanted by him, Doris, until he put you squarely in your place.'

Doris Frobisher seethed and would have retorted strongly, but she could not afford to risk offending Maude Briggs.

'Don't you think we have had quite enough of Lady Grantwell's vicissitudes?' asked Sylvia Charnford. 'Apart from her title, what else does she have to offer? I propose we support the rector.'

'And I second that proposition,' added Martin Bell.

'All in favour?' queried the rector.

A show of hands gave a majority of nine votes to three in favour of the motion.

As the meeting was breaking up, Sylvia Charnford drew Martin Bell aside and gave him her son's message requesting that he would call at The Chequers. George Turley accompanied Martin as far as the inn.

'I'm calling in here to see someone,' Martin said. 'I don't suppose you're coming in, George?'

'I am not!' the grocer retorted with a show of distaste.

'Well, I'll bid you goodnight then,' said Martin and he disappeared inside the hostelry without awaiting any further reply.

Martin made his way through the crowded bar to where the two younger men were sitting awaiting his arrival.

'What will you have Mr Bell?' Chris asked him after he had shaken hands with them and taken a seat.

'A half of lager will be just right,' he said.

When Chris returned with the drink he asked, 'Did the meeting go well?'

'Very well,' Martin replied, and to Rolf he said, 'We were delighted to hear that you are going to open the fête for us, Mr Muller.'

Rolf made no reply to this observation, but instead he asked, 'How is Mrs Bell?'

'The doctor was quite pleased with her today,' Martin said, 'but he never seems to see her when she is at her lowest ebb. Sometimes she can go for a week without any sign of pain, and then it comes on again quite suddenly. How much longer she's going to be able to bear it, I just don't know.'

Rolf leaned over towards him and said, very quietly, 'If you will accept the suggestion I'm going to make to you, it may not be too long. My father is an eminent rheumatologist, and has performed numerous successful operations on arthritic patients. I have been speaking with him this evening and providing you and your wife are in agreement, he is willing to accept her into his clinic in Germany during the first week in September.' A look of disbelief, and then a glimmer of hope began to light up his face, to be followed immediately by a feeling of anguish. Fate, how could you be so cruel; why am I being so tormented?

A look of despair disfigured his whole countenance as he cried out, 'But I couldn't possibly raise enough money.'

Rolf looked him squarely in the face and said, 'There will be no need for you to raise any money.'

Martin look searchingly into the eyes of the young German, and with tears rolling down his cheeks he choked, 'Oh, bless you; bless you.'

Another drink was out of the question; Martin couldn't wait to get home to give Grace the wonderful news. He asked Rolf and Chris to come with him to corroborate what he had to tell her. She would have all sorts of questions to ask, and Martin couldn't trust himself to fill her in on the details. Arriving at his cottage, Martin fitted his key in the lock and opening the door he cried out, 'I'm home, dear. I've brought two friends to see you.'

'Really,' thought Grace, 'how inconsiderate of you, Martin, to bring people here at this time of night.' But when she saw young Mr Muller, her attitude changed to one of pleasure.

'Hello, Mr Muller; how kind of you to come.'

She did not recognise his companion, and waited for an introduction to be made. As no introduction was forthcoming, she looked quizzically at Chris who smiled and said, 'Don't you know me Mrs Bell? You taught me at Sunday School.'

She continued to look at him until recognition came to her, and she said, 'You're Daphne's brother.'

'That's right, Mrs Bell; I'm Christopher.'

Grace chuckled and said, 'Daphne came to see me this morning; what a lovely young lady she is, to be sure.'

Any further talk on the subject of Daphne Charnford was cut short by Martin who announced, 'I've got some wonderful news for you, Grace. Mr Muller has arranged for you to go to Germany to have treatment for your arthritis.'

She looked at her husband and quietly said, 'What do you mean. What are you talking about?'

It was not like Martin to play tricks on her; what, she wondered, had prompted this cruel hoax.

'You'd better tell her, Mr Muller,' said Martin and drawing Chris aside he took him into another room, leaving Rolf to talk to his wife.

'Mrs Bell, I didn't mention it when I was with you yesterday, but my father is director of the Lintzen Clinic in Germany. He specialises in rheumatology, and has successfully treated numerous cases of arthritis. I can say modestly that he is amongst the leading authorities in Europe in his particular field. I do not make any rash promises, but I can assure you that you could not possibly put yourself in better hands. I spoke with him this evening and he has agreed to take you, provided you can go there on the third of September.'

'The first question you will want to ask,' said Rolf, 'is how can you afford to pay? The answer to that is, there will be nothing to pay. The next question will be, how do you get to Germany? To that question, the answer is, I shall be returning to Germany by car and ferry, and I can take you with me. I shall arrange for a nurse to travel with us. The nurse will be someone you know; Miss Daphne Charnford.'

'It may sound strange to you, Mr Muller, but I can't let you do it; we couldn't possibly repay you; but thank you so much for the offer. I shall always remember your kindness.'

The response did not in any way surprise Rolf. One of the characteristics of Grace Bell that had first struck him was her strong independent spirit, and so he resisted any argument. Instead he said, 'Please Mrs Bell, don't make up your mind immediately. I'll call on you again on Saturday, and when you've had more time to think it over you can give me your final decision.'

'Very well, Mr Muller' she replied, 'but I tell you, it will be no different from what it is now.'

Martin and Chris returned to Mrs Bell and the young German, and the look of disappointment on Rolf's face told them everything.

'If you'll excuse me, I'll be going to my bed,' Grace said.

Martin went to assist her, and he asked the two young men to wait until he had attended to his wife's requirements. While they were alone, Rolf told Chris of Mrs Bell's reaction to his proposal, and Chris was ready to sympathise with him, but Rolf made it clear that he was not going to accept the refusal without a struggle.

Chris suggested to Rolf that Martin should be taken into his confidence concerning his interest in The Park.

'Yes, Chris,' Rolf said, 'and I think also that we should let your family know just what we are doing.'

Martin came down the stairs looking most disconsolate, and he muttered, 'I'm sorry Mr Muller; I just don't know what to say.'

'Don't be concerned,' Rolf said; 'we have until Saturday to make a decision. Many things can happen before then.'

'There is another matter we'd like to discuss,' Chris put in.

'Rolf is trying to contact the families of some of the workmen who were employed on the Maresfield Park estate when the First World War broke out. If you think it would not be putting too great a strain on your father, we'd like to go to see him and ask him if can remember the names of any of these men.'

Turning to Rolf, Martin said, 'If it will help you in any way, Mr Muller, I'll be happy to take you to see him tomorrow. It will be good for him to feel that he can be useful to somebody.'

'We'd appreciate it,' Chris said, 'if you didn't mention to anyone the fact that we are making these inquiries. There isn't time tonight to go into why we want to know their names, but confidentiality is of the utmost importance.'

'You have no need to tell me anything more,' Martin said. 'I can be ready by ten o'clock tomorrow morning, so if you will call for me, we can go together.'

14

On Thursday morning the Charnford family took breakfast together. That in itself was unique. When they were all seated, Chris casually remarked,

'Rolf asked me to fill you in a little more fully on his reasons for coming to Maresfield. Apparently, somewhere in The Park there may be a chest lying hidden since the year 1914. Rolf's great-grandfather is thought to have had it buried there by workmen at the outbreak of the first war. He has no idea what it may contain but his grandfather, who was just a child at the time, saw it being buried, and told Rolf about it. Just before he died, he made Rolf promise that he would come to England and seek it out.'

'In which part of The Park is it supposed to be buried?' Mrs Charnford asked.

'The only clue he has is that there are, or were, five oak trees nearby and that, as you can imagine, is no clue at all when you consider all the oaks there must have been before The Park was developed into a housing estate. Kitty's father has been very helpful in letting him have sight of the plans for the first stages of development. He's been able to establish from these plans which properties had trees left on them, although they may not necessarily be oaks.'

Arthur Charnford remained silent for a few minutes before he joined in the conversation.

'I wonder if that can in some way account for the strange goings on in The Park over the past few months.'

'You mean the holes being dug on Commander Brewster's property?' queried Daphne.

'And one or two others,' said her father. 'It looks as though Rolf is not the only one who is interested.'

Chris warned the family of the need for secrecy and Daphne, looking just a little pale, asked, 'Rolf isn't in any kind of danger, is he?'

Chris laughed and said jokingly, 'Good heavens no, Daph. He just wants to be the first to get his hands on the treasure.'

After breakfast was over, Chris walked out towards the stables with his father to discuss some of the jobs that required to be seen to during the day. The sound of whinnying coming from the direction of Vincent's stall caused Chris to go over and pat the horse on the head and allow himself to be nuzzled. 'Not today old chap,' he said, and to his father he remarked, 'It looks as though I'm going to have a fairly busy morning with Rolf. When we've got the men moving, I'll be off. I expect to be home by lunchtime.'

When Chris arrived at The Chequers he found Rolf talking with Charles Broxon. It was clear to Chris that Charles was agitated, and so he stood aside to allow them to finish their conversation. As soon as Rolf noticed him however, he drew him in and said, 'Chris, take a look at this will you?'

He handed Chris a piece of paper on which had been scribbled,

'Fritz, go home if you know what's good for you.'

'I found this when I returned to my room last night,' said Rolf, 'it had been pushed under my door.'

'I'll get to the bottom of this,' declared Charles. 'I just can't say how sorry I am that this should have happened.'

'Please Charles, take no notice,' said Rolf, 'I have no intention of being intimidated.'

Chris turned to the innkeeper, 'Have you any ideas, Charles?'

'I won't jump to any hasty conclusions,' said Charles, 'although I have one or two ideas. I'm puzzled as to how they knew which was Rolf's room, but just leave it with me; I'll get to the bottom of it before the day's out.'

Rolf and Chris climbed into the Jaguar and set off to pick up Martin Bell. As they drove past the village petrol station, a battered old navy blue Ford Consul pulled out of the forecourt and fell in behind them. Chris chuckled slightly as he said to Rolf, 'It beats me how such a car could possibly have passed the MOT.'

Rolf was puzzled and so Chris explained to him that he was referring to the certificate of roadworthiness. Looking into his mirror Chris took a mental note of the registration number, 33 EXT, observing, 'The car must be older than the owner.'

Leaving the main road, they drove into a cul-de-sac, at the end of which stood Martin's cottage. Martin was already at his gate when they arrived, and lost no time in climbing in behind them. Chris reversed the car towards the main road and pointed it again in the direction of the village. Out of the corner of his eye he could see the old Ford with its bonnet raised, and the driver looking down at the engine. As soon as the Jaguar was on the main road, the driver of the Ford slammed down the bonnet and leapt into the car, did a quick U turn and proceeded to follow them.

Seeing all this in his driving mirror, Chris muttered to his companions, 'Don't look round; we're being followed.'

He drove on in silence for a couple of minutes and then said,

'I shall drive on through the village as far as Lampool Corner. I shall turn right and drive towards the forest for a short distance and give him a chance to overtake us.'

Chris turned at Lampool, drove on past the Fairwarp turning, and on towards the open forest. Then he slowed down to a crawl, leaving his pursuer no alternative but to overtake. The Ford picked up speed until it was out of sight, and Chris outlined his plan of action.

'There's a secluded gateway round the next bend in the road, and just beyond that there's a road junction. I should guess that he will be waiting in the gateway in order to see which road we take. What I propose to do is to drive across the entrance and block him in; then we'll have a word with him and find out what he's up to. Are you with me?'

As Chris had predicted, the Ford Consul was standing well back in the gateway, its engine still running, nose towards the road, ready to take up pursuit. He drove the Jaguar squarely across its bows, cutting off any possible retreat. Chris and Rolf jumped out, and together they closed in on the old car. Pulling open the driver's door, they unceremoniously yanked him out of his seat and onto his feet on the grass outside. He stood glaring defiantly at them for a time, and then he broke down and began to sob convulsively. They saw for the first time that he was little more than a boy, and Chris felt his initial anger turn to pity. He gave the youth time to compose himself before asking, 'Now, what are you up to?'

A frightened Cockney voice said, 'I d'know wot yer mean; I aint done nuffin'.'

'Why are you following us?' Chris demanded to know.

'I aint follerin' yer; honest I aint,' the lad said.

Martin came over towards him and gently asked the young man,

'What is your name?'

'I aint tellin' yer,' was the resolute reply.

'Very well then,' Martin said, 'empty your pockets.'

Again there was a stubborn reluctance to comply, and Chris interposed, 'We don't want to hurt you, but if you don't do as we say we may have to. Or would you prefer that we hand you over to the police?'

'No! don't do that, guv'nor; please don't do that.'

'Then do as we say,' insisted Chris.

The lad began slowly and reluctantly to empty his pockets, starting with those in his trousers. There was little of interest; some loose change, a grubby handkerchief, and from the rear pocket he produced a leather wallet containing fifty pounds in new five pound notes.

His windcheater jacket proved more interesting, and he needed some persuasion before he revealed the contents. Eventually, he took the jacket off and produced an amazing assortment of weaponry. There was a regulation style police truncheon, a flick knife, a knuckleduster, a nylon stocking; a second wallet containing five Barclay cards, a driving licence in the name of Richard Fledham, and twenty pounds in cash. There was also a cheap notepad with bold blue lines across its sheets. A crumpled business card dropped to the ground; only Chris seemed to notice it. He picked it up and read, P R Frobisher,

Dealer in Antiques, Export/Import, 13 Beadle Street, Hackney, London E7. Unobserved by the youth, Chris slipped it into his pocket.

Martin examined the driving licence and noticed that there were two endorsements, but it was the notepad which took Rolf's attention. Taking a pencil from his pocket, he told the youth to write on a page of the pad: 'Fritz, go home if you know what's good for you.'

The youth refused, and Rolf did not press the matter, but slipped the pad into his own pocket.

Chris in turn examined the driving licence and made a note of the boy's address, '19 Cheyne Rise, Hackney, London E7.' He then took the ignition key from the Ford and opened up the boot. Inside the boot were three spades, a metal detector, a balaclava helmet, some sacking material, an assortment of clothing, including a pair of stout boots and a pair of long thick woollen socks. Chris lifted the sacking to reveal a shotgun with a shortened barrel. Turning again to the youngster he said, 'You either tell us all we want to know, or we hand you over to the police. Now first, what is your name?'

'Richard Fledham,' he replied.

'And your address?'

'19 Cheyne Rise, Hackney.'

'Is this your own car?' Chris continued.

'Yes.'

'Who put you up to all this?'

'I d' know wot yer mean,' the youth said.

'Now come on; out with it, or we'll let the police deal with you.
Now, who are you working for?'

'Please, guv'nor, if I tell yer, yer won't shop me, will yer?' the lad wailed.

'Not unless we have to,' Chris promised, 'but that all depends on you, and how deeply you are implicated.'

'I get mi orders from annuver geezer wot works up in London, but 'e don't know much neever.'

'And are you absolutely sure you don't know who is behind it all?'

'Absolutely, guv'nor; cross mi 'eart,' he wailed.

'When will you be meeting him again?' Chris persisted.

'Eight o'clock tonight; church car park; but I aint gonna be there; straight up I aint.'

Seeing that the game was up, the youth decided to throw himself on their mercy and make a clean breast of everything. His name, he told them was Private Alan Pattaway. He was on the run from the army, having assaulted his adjutant. He had escaped from his military escort while on his way to court martial, and made for London. There, he had lived on his wits for three months, doing odd jobs in various clip joints and similar establishments in the Soho district. He had met up with a man whom he knew only as Ned. Ned had taken him to a 'safe' place which had turned out to be a thieves' kitchen. It was a real homely place, with plenty to eat and a bed to sleep on. At first he had been foolish enough to think that he was the guest of a genuine benefactor, but after two weeks 'the guv'nor' paid a call to interview newcomers.

Young Pattaway was left in no doubt regarding his obligations; he was given the choice of drug pushing, or of joining 'The heavies'. The thought of handling drugs frightened him, and so he had opted for 'the heavies'.

'Up to now,' he said, 'all I've 'ad ter do was ter drive mi motor. They told me ter come dahn 'ere an' join the 'country squad'. I've got meself lodgin's in Crawley an' mi landlord finks I'm workin' on the airport at Gatwick.'

Martin interposed, 'What is your address in Crawley, Alan?'

Reluctantly the answer was given, '27 Iveson Way.'

'What activities are you engaged in here?' Chris asked him.

'Just markin' time. I'm gettin' mi orders from a geezer wot I meet in the church car park.'

'And how long have you been getting these orders?'

'Larst night was the first time. All 'e told me ter do was ter keep tabs on this 'ere geezer,' he nodded towards Rolf, 'then I was ter report back abaht where 'e went an' 'oo 'e was with.'

Rolf put the note in front of the youth and said, 'Was this written by you?'

'Yes,' the lad admitted, 'but I didn't mean nuffin' by it.'

Rolf didn't press the point, feeling there was nothing to

be gained from it, but Chris asked him, 'How did you know which door to put it under?'

The lad touched his closely pressed lips with his finger, indicating that he was not telling.

Calling Martin and Rolf to one side, Chris quietly said, 'Rolf, you can see the entrance to the church car park from your bedroom window. I propose we let him keep his rendezvous this evening, and we can watch without being observed, and discover who is giving him his orders.' Rolf readily agreed on this line of action, and the youth was told he could go, but he was to keep his eight o'clock appointment, and tell his contact that he had shadowed the German as far as the M25 motorway at South Goddesden and seen him take the London bound carriageway. He was also to take further instructions, if possible for a longer period. After receiving his instructions, he was to contact Mr Muller and let him have details of them. A note under his door would suffice.

Leaving the youth to fill in the rest of the day as he would, the three men took to the car and resumed their journey via the woodland road through Nutley village, arriving at Rockwood a little later than they had planned. Old Isaac Bell was waiting patiently in his room as Martin went in ahead of the others. A few goodies were handed over, but the old man paid little attention to them; his mind was elsewhere.

'What about the young German lad?' he said. 'When's he comin' to see me?'

'Be patient, Father' Martin said, 'he's waiting outside. There's another young man with him. I don't suppose you'll remember him: Chris Charnford.'

'You mean Charnford from the Livery Stables? 'course I remember 'im; but 'is name weren't Chris; it were Arthur.'

'No, Father; Chris is Arthur's son,' Martin said patiently. A faraway look came over the elderly blacksmith's face as he said, 'e were a great 'orseman were young Arthur.'

Martin cut short his father's reminiscences by opening the door and asking the two young men to step inside the room. Rolf led the way and was greeted warmly by old

Isaac. Chris remained in the background until eventually Martin managed to persuade his father to meet his other visitor. Isaac looked at Chris and declared, 'This 'ere's Arthur Charnford.'

Chris shook hands with the old gentleman and said, 'It's good to see you, Mr Bell,' and to Martin, 'What's in a name?'

Martin waited for a lull in the conversation before saying, 'Mr Muller would like you to help him, Father.'

His father nodded his head eagerly, and looking at Rolf he said, 'I'll 'elp you all I can.'

'Thank you, sir' said Rolf. 'I'm trying to discover the names of all the gardeners and general labourers who were employed by Prince Munster at the time when the First War broke out.'

'Most of 'em is long sin' put away,' Isaac told him. 'I were just a little 'un at t' time.'

'It's just the names I need, Mr Bell, so that I can trace their families,' said Rolf. 'If you can give me one or two names now, and then perhaps let me know some others when you have had time to think of them, I shall be most grateful.'

Many a younger man than Isaac would have been greatly exercised to remember names from as far back as seventy years, but he immediately came out with three of them: Tom Leaming, Joe Readman, Eli Parkin. 'Eli is still livin' wi' 'is son somewhere in Nutley; th' other two 'ave bin gone a long time. Then there were Adam Fawcett. What 'appened to Adam?'

Martin felt that his father was tiring and so he suggested that they ought to go. The old man was reluctant for them to leave, but a bell sounded to let him know that lunch was being served and they were able to depart without causing him any distress.

15

When Rolf returned to *The Chequers* he was handed a message from the Reverend P. Truscott.

'Would Mr Muller be so kind as to make a call at the rectory as soon as he was able to spare the time.'

Rolf saw no point in keeping the reverend gentleman waiting; he made his way into The Park and was welcomed by Mrs Truscott.

'Good afternoon,' said the lady. 'Please come inside; my husband should be back at any moment. Will you have a cup of tea?' She didn't wait for an answer, but carried on talking. 'Do take a seat. Isn't it a beautiful day. I do hope you're enjoying your stay in Maresfield.'

The rector arrived in time to prevent his wife running out of steam.

'Thank you for coming so promptly,' the rector said. 'I want to put you in the picture about the garden fête. Colonel and Mrs Briggs have very kindly agreed that we should hold it at The Limes; we have held it there over the past three years and it has proved very satisfactory. The time of opening will be 10.30 and Mrs Briggs is providing coffee for members of the committee and yourself. If you can help to judge the fancy dress competition, that will be greatly appreciated. The fancy dress parade will leave Parklands at a quarter to ten and will be led by the Lewes Venturers' Carnival Band. Lunch for members of the committee and the official opening party will be at one o'clock in the small marquee. After lunch it is customary for the celebrity to pay a visit to each of the stalls. I hope you will not find this too onerous a task.'

Rolf expressed his pleasure at being able to comply with the requirements of his brief hour of distinction, and said he had a favour to ask of the rector.

'It concerns Mrs Bell,' he said. 'I had the pleasure of meeting this sweet lady earlier this week.'

Before he could proceed, the rector burst in, 'Oh dear, oh dear, Mr Muller; you have pricked my conscience. I'm afraid I've badly neglected her over the past two or three weeks.'

'Yes,' persisted Rolf, 'I'm not concerned about anything but her health, and this is where you may be able to help. My father, who is a leading authority on rheumatology, has offered to take Mrs Bell into his clinic in Germany, but I have so far been unable to persuade her to take up the offer. She is a very independent lady and declines to have outside help for which she can not pay.'

'And how would you assess her chances of recovery?' asked the rector.

'It would be foolish of me to attempt a prognosis,' Rolf declared, 'but I have every confidence in my father.'

'How does Martin Bell feel about it?'

'When I put it to him he was delighted,' said Rolf, 'but now he is bitterly disappointed at his wife's reluctance.'

'I shall lose no time in going to see her,' the rector said. 'We'll just have our cup of tea and then, if you'll excuse me, I'll be on my way.'

Rolf felt that in Daphne Charnford he had another ally and, leaving the rectory, he took a walk in the direction of the Livery Stables. Daphne came to the door in answer to his knock. She greeted him with a cheery, 'Hello, Rolf, how nice to see you, but I'm afraid Chris isn't at home. There's no one here but me.'

'It's you I want to see, Daphne, if you can spare the time. May I walk a little in the garden with you?'

'I've loads of time if you have,' she replied. 'Why don't we take a walk on the forest? It's such a beautiful day. I'll get my car and we'll take a run as far as King's Standing and park it there.'

'Why not!' Rolf enthused.

As they drove the short distance onto Ashdown Forest few words were exchanged, but as soon as they left the car Rolf said, 'I'm afraid my plans for Mrs Bell have suffered a setback.'

'Do you mean your father can't accept her after all?'
Daphne made no attempt to hide her dismay.

'No, it's not that,' Rolf replied. 'It's Mrs Bell herself; she
is declining the invitation to go to Germany.'

'I might have know she would; she's so independent.
What does Mr Bell have to say about it?'

'He's very disappointed, but he doesn't wish to distress
her. I have told him they have until Saturday to make a
final decision. I've advised Mr Truscott about the
situation and he is going to see Mrs Bell this afternoon.'

'Would it be any use my going to see her, Rolf?'

'I was rather hoping you would, but might I suggest a
little innocent subtlety. If she could be persuaded that you
would be disappointed at missing the opportunity of
going to Germany, it might encourage her a little. Do you
think you could pretend to be disappointed?'

'I should be very disappointed,' declared Daphne, 'and
that would be no pretence, I can assure you. I shall
certainly call and see her.'

They walked on together for half a mile, talking
trivialities. Daphne asked Rolf one or two questions about
his family, and he gave her a thumbnail sketch of life in
Langentopf.

'My home,' he said, 'is on the River Elbe about fifty
kilometres from Hamburg. It is not by any means the
most beautiful part of Germany, but yet it is very
interesting. Blankenese, which is a little way down river, is
a most picturesque little town with fine houses and
gardens towering over the river. Beyond is the small town
of Wedel-Schulau which is well-known to sailors from all
over the world. It has a famous riverside café from which
all passing ships are hailed as they pass on their way to
and from the harbour at Hamburg, and whatever the
ship's nationality, the appropriate national anthem is
played. Hamburg itself is a very busy port, but it is also a
very beautiful city.'

He glanced at Daphne to make sure he wasn't boring
her.

'Germany, as I'm sure you must know, is a country of
very great contrasts. Most people flock to Bavaria, The
Harz Mountains, The Black Forest or The Rhine Valley,

but there is so much beauty in Schleswig Holstein, and even in such areas as The Ruhr Valley, which is the industrial heart of Germany, there are some beautiful sights to be seen.'

Daphne found herself being caught up in Rolf's tremendous enthusiasm, and without conscious thought she whispered, 'Please let me come with you.' It was said so innocently, as if to herself. Before Rolf could respond her mood suddenly changed, and she began to talk about her own country.

'You must see more of England, Rolf, and, of course Scotland, and Wales and Ireland. You must see the Lake District and the North Yorkshire Moors and Dales with their ancient monasteries and castles. Visit some of our ancient cities: Canterbury, Oxford, York and Cambridge.' She carried on talking, knowing that any break in the conversation might lead to a compromising response to what she now thought of as her indiscretion. They walked on in a circle, returning after an hour to where the car was parked. Rolf wanted desperately to ask her out again but he couldn't bear a refusal. He felt perhaps it would be better to leave it until he had some definite sign of encouragement from Daphne. After all he had been in England less than a week.

When she had driven Rolf back to The Chequers, Daphne did not return home immediately; instead she made her way to the Bells' cottage. She arrived just as the rector was leaving. He raised his hat and wished her good afternoon. From the expression on his face she could detect nothing of either success or failure in his mission, and so she was a little apprehensive as she tapped on the front door and called out, 'It's Daphne Charnford, Mrs Bell.'

'Oh, do come along in, my dear; I wasn't expecting to see you again quite so soon.' The voice was as friendly as ever, but Daphne thought she detected a note of weariness. 'I'm in a bit of a turmoil; people are so very kind. That lovely young German gentleman arranging for me to go to his father's clinic in Germany; it's all too much; I couldn't possibly put people to so much trouble.'

'But, Mrs Bell, you've no idea of the pleasure it would

give Mr Muller to do this for you. He's such a fine man, and you've made a tremendous impression on him. It would be so wonderful for Mr Bell too, if you could be cured. Think of all the things you would be able to do together. Please, Mrs Bell, why don't you put your pride behind you and accept the offer?'

Mrs Bell bridled somewhat at Daphne's reference to her pride.

'Do you really think it's pride my dear? I assure you it is not. But who am I that I should be taking up the valuable time of people like Mr Muller? and, of course, there's you too, Daphne. Oh yes, I heard that you had very kindly offered to give up your holiday time in order to travel with me. I shall never forget your willingness to sacrifice your own pleasure so that you could help me. I can't let you do it.'

'Mrs Bell,' said Daphne, 'you obviously have no idea of the tremendous assistance that your Martin and his father have been to Mr Muller. Had it not been for their willingness to help him, his visit to England would have been a complete waste of time. As for myself, I'm making no sacrifice whatsoever. I want very much to go to Germany, and I saw this as a heaven-sent opportunity to be useful, and at the same time to take a holiday I could not otherwise afford.'

Grace looked searchingly into Daphne's eyes and said, 'Are you quite sure of what you are saying, my dear?'

Daphne assured her, 'I'm quite certain, Mrs Bell.'

'And has Martin really been able to help Mr Muller?'

Daphne nodded.

'And are you really going to be able to make it a holiday?'

'Yes, of course I am,' Daphne said. 'Once we've got you safely to the clinic you will be in very capable hands, and I shall have no more duties until you are ready to come home.'

Grace began slowly to nod her head, and a beautiful smile came over her face as she said, 'Then I shall go to Germany.'

Shortly after seven o'clock in the evening, Chris called round at The Chequers and went up to join Rolf in his room.

'It looks as though my clever little sister has pulled it off,' said Chris.

'Pulled it off?' Rolf was puzzled. 'What do you mean, Chris?'

'She's persuaded Mrs Bell to go to Germany with you.'

'Hoorah!' cried Rolf in an uncharacteristic display of fervour.

'Now she can have her holiday.'

Chris was in a jovial mood, and could not resist a little leg-pulling. He said, 'Hey, I thought the object of the exercise was to find a cure for Mrs Bell's ailments.'

Rolf felt his cheeks going red with embarrassment and could think of no suitable response, but Chris relented and said, 'Seriously, Rolf, I think it's a fine thing that you are doing and I'm happy for Martin as well as for Mrs Bell.'

It was a quarter to eight when looking through the bedroom window, Rolf and Chris observed the battered old Ford Consul entering the church car park. They had a perfect view of the car park entrance, but as the car moved further in towards the rear it was lost to their view. All they had to do was to keep an eye on the entrance to see who it was who was coming to meet young Pattaway. They watched patiently for half an hour, but saw no one else enter the car park. The only sign of movement was when eventually the young man walked out of the car park and went towards the front entrance of The Chequers.

Two or three minutes later they heard a stealthy movement in the passageway outside Rolf's door, and then they saw a slip of paper appearing under the door. As quick as a flash Chris leapt forward, opened the door and grabbed a startled young Alan Pattaway and dragged him unceremoniously inside the room. Rolf closed the door behind them; Chris released his hold on the youth and gave him time to recover from the shock.

'Now my lad,' Chris said, 'just what do you think you're up to?'

'I aint up to nuffin', guv. I did exac'ly wot yer told me. I met the geezer in the car park an' I brought yer the note abaht it.'

'What do you take us for?' Chris demanded. 'We saw you drive into the car park, and no one else went anywhere near. We were watching the whole time and no other car came anywhere near the car park.'

''ere, just a minute, guv'nor; I didn' say nuffin' abaht a car; 'e never came in no car; 'e was walkin'.'

Rolf interrupted; 'But no one walked into the car park!'

Then it began to dawn on Chris that they had overlooked a vital point.

'Of course,' he said; 'there's a footpath leading straight through into The Park. Is that the way he came into the car park?'

'Yer it is,' the youth said, 'an' if yer'll read mi note yer'll find aht wot 'e said ter mi: an' yer don't need ter spy on mi neiver.'

Rolf read the note which said simply, 'Got to go to Hackney to take some stuff.'

He handed the slip of paper to Chris who glanced at it and said,

'What address in Hackney?'

'13 Beadle Street.'

'Where is the stuff coming from?' Chris asked.

'I'm meetin' two blokes on a lay-by opposite Piltdown Pond at ten o'clock tomorrer mornin'.'

'I'm sorry we doubted you, Alan,' Chris said.

''sorl right, guv, but wot am I gonna do abaht it?'

Chris looked at Rolf and said, 'I propose he goes ahead and does as instructed. What to you think ?'

'I agree,' said Rolf.

Chris then said to Alan, 'Do as we tell you, and we'll find some way of getting you out of the mess you're in. In the meantime, carry on taking your orders, but be sure to let us know well in advance what those orders are. And now, how would you like some food?'

'That 'ud be great, guv'nor.'

Chris said to Rolf, 'I'll pop down and ask Pat Broxon what she can do for us.'

When he returned he brought with him a tray with glasses and a bottle of wine.

'Pat has put a lasagne in the microwave oven,' he said. 'It should be ready in about ten minutes.'

When the food came, young Pattaway gave a creditable performance in helping to put it away in record time. He was ready for a second helping before the others had started.

After the lad had left them Chris said to Rolf, 'You're seeing the Colbeys tomorrow morning I believe. What time do you have to be there?'

'No particular time was mentioned, but I thought of going around half past ten. What do you have in mind?'

'I thought of taking a walk across Piltdown Golf Course. One of the fairways comes pretty close to Piltdown Pond, and the trees there will provide a first-class observation post. I'll be able to see just what happens at the lay-by. You go to the Colbeys as arranged, and might I suggest we meet at The Peacock for a light lunch? Dad tells me you are riding in the afternoon. Sorry I can't be with you, but I've arranged to go out with Kitty.'

'Don't take any risks, Chris,' Rolf said. 'Sorry I can't be there with you, but I look forward to hearing from you. I'll be at The Peacock as near to twelve o'clock as I can make it.'

16

On the Friday morning, Rolf had a leisurely breakfast, and afterwards he took a walk down to the village shop to make a few small purchases. George Turley was busy serving customers, and there were one or two others waiting for attention. As soon as he saw the young German, he called through to his wife to come and give some assistance. George would have turned his back on the other customers, had not Rolf insisted on awaiting his turn to be served. When at last Mr Turley was able to attend to him he said to Rolf,

'Good morning, sir. What can I get for you?' Before Rolf had time to reply, he continued, 'I'm so glad the rector managed to persuade you to open the Garden Fête.'

'It's very kind of you to say so, Mr Turley. May I have the items on this list, please?'

Chris, in the meantime, had parked his Jaguar outside The Peacock, and made his way on foot up to the golf course. It was a beautiful clear morning and there were several golfers on the course. Although one or two of these were known to Chris, most of them were strangers. Fortunately, they were too engrossed in their game to notice him as he made his way stealthily among the trees, carefully avoiding the open ground of the fairways. As he was approaching a clump of hawthorne, he saw a man training a pair of binoculars on an object on the far side of the pond. Chris managed to avoid being seen by the man, but was near enough to recognise him as Peter Frobisher.

He realised that there was no way he could approach the vantage point he had aimed for without being seen. There was no alternative for him but to retrace his footsteps. Without wasting any further time, he returned

to *The Peacock* and picked up the Jaguar. He made for
The Chequers, hoping to be in time to intercept Rolf on
his way to the Colbeys. Fortune was on his side as he made
his way into the car park at the rear of the inn. Rolf was
just leaving by the rear door, and was surprised to see his
friend.

'We'll have to change our plans, Rolf,' said Chris.

He told Rolf of his failure to observe the happenings at
Piltdown but Rolf felt that Chris's journey had been well
worth the effort as it confirmed the suspicion they had
both been harbouring relative to the activities of Peter
Frobisher.

'I won't hold you up now,' Chris said, 'but let's meet at
The Chequers instead of at *The Peacock*. Don't tie
yourself down to any particular time, but I'll be there at
twelve o'clock.' They went their respective ways, both
turning over in their minds what they had discovered,
and wondering how best to exploit their newly gathered
information.

Rolf felt at home with the Colbeys; they were mature
people, with a natural, easy charm. He was, however,
aware of a slight uneasiness in their manner as they met
him at the door, but this was soon dispelled when the two
men were alone.

'Beryl's just gone to put the coffee on to percolate,'
Roger said, 'shall we take a short walk until it's ready?'

They walked out onto a terrace at the rear of the house,
and over a wide expanse of lawn towards a massive
greenhouse with a vine laden with bunches of black
grapes. As they drew closer, an elderly gardener
approached them bearing a basket of runner beans which
he was taking to the house.

'Good morning, Hopkins,' said Mr Colbey, 'is the
greenhouse open?'

'Mornin', sir,' replied Hopkins. 'No it still be closed; I
just finished fillin' in the last o' the 'oles.'

Hopkins continued on his way, and Roger explained,

'You'll remember what I was saying the other evening
at the Briggs'; I told you we'd had people round with
metal detectors. I'm afraid I didn't tell you all that had
happened; Hopkins discovered half a dozen holes in

among the trees. I didn't care to discuss the matter with my neighbours, and so I kept my own counsel. Quite frankly, I'm worried; I suppose I should have informed the police, but I just couldn't bear the thought of police patrol cars chasing about all over the place and disturbing the neighbourhood. One can be made to look a bit of a fool. If they attempted to break into the house of course, that would be a totally different matter. Whoever would want to be digging holes on my land I can't imagine, and what could they possibly hope to find?'

They were still within earshot of the house, and Beryl Colbey had no difficulty in making herself heard when she called, 'Roger, will you come now and have coffee?'

Once inside the house, Mrs Colbey took over the conversation.

'I hope you are enjoying your stay in Maresfield, Mr Muller.'

'Yes, Mrs Colbey, I am,' said Rolf. 'Most of the people I have met have been very kind. It's hard to realise that I have been here less than one week.'

'We hear very little of local gossip,' said Beryl, 'for which I suppose we should be thankful, but we heard on the local radio that you'd had an adventure when you left the Briggs' house on Tuesday evening.'

Rolf was clearly embarrassed and attempted to shrug it off, but the lady persisted; 'What you did was a very brave act and one which I regret is all too rare amongst our local population. We are having quite a spate of criminal activity in the area. The police are doing their best to keep it under control, but it is more than they can be expected to do when there are so many incidents to deal with. Roger and I were hoping to go up to London for a day or two next week with my sister, but it looks as though we shall have to cancel it. One just can't leave one's home unattended.'

Roger joined in, observing, 'I suppose we could always engage security guards, but it seems so pretentious and only serves to draw attention to oneself.'

An idea began to form in Rolf's mind, and he said to Mr Colbey, 'Do you know the Charnford family?'

'Yes, of course, we know them quite well,' said Roger,

'delightful people, but why do you ask?'

'How would it be if Chris Charnford and I undertook to keep an eye on your home for two nights next week? I'm sure Chris won't mind, and I'd be very pleased to help.'

'Oh, Mr Muller; what a splendid idea,' enthused Mrs Colbey, 'but wouldn't that be imposing too much on you?'

'Not at all, Mrs Colbey; I'm seeing Chris this afternoon and I'll put the idea to him. Now which days do you wish to be away?'

'If we go on Tuesday and come back on Thursday, that will mean two nights away from home, Tuesday and Wednesday,' said Beryl.

'I'll let you know this afternoon what Chris says about it,' Rolf promised.

'Daphne Charnford has been here quite often,' Mrs Colbey said. 'My niece Helen spends at least three weeks with us each summer, and Daphne and Kitty Prewett usually get together with her when she comes. She hasn't been this year; I suspect there's a boy somewhere in the picture. You've met Daphne, I suppose?'

'Yes, I have,' Rolf said, and Beryl Colbey didn't fail to notice the expression on his face as he said it.

The morning passed quite pleasantly, and with no mention being made of the subject which had prompted Roger Colbey to invite Rolf to his home. Beryl suggested that the young man might care to stay and share a light lunch with them, but Rolf asked to be excused as he had already made other arrangements.

When he arrived at The Chequers, Rolf was pleasantly surprised to see Daphne and Kitty sitting there alongside Chris.

'I hope you don't mind having company,' Chris said apologetically.

'Oh no; this is perfectly delightful,' Rolf said as he reached over to shake hands with Kitty and then, at conspicuously greater length, with Daphne.

There were relatively few customers in The Chequers, and Charles and Pat Broxon were able to spend a considerable time with them. They were determined to impress their guests, which was clearly evident by the way of lightheartedness at the table, and Rolf was particularly exhilarated by the feeling he had of being a part of the family.

He was hesitant about changing the tone of the conversation by reference to his visit to the Colbeys but, remembering his promise to the elderly couple, he told the others of their reticence to leave their home unattended overnight, and of how disappointed they were at being unable to go up to London to visit Mrs Colbey's sister. He told them also of the mysterious incident of the holes dug in the ground. This brought an immediate response from Chris.

'We've got to do something, Rolf; we can't allow a dear old couple like the Colbeys to be terrorised, which is what it amounts to. I suppose, to be fair to the police, there's not much they can do until something big happens, by which time, the damage will have been done.'

'Mr Colbey is reluctant to call in the police,' Rolf said, 'but what I have suggested is that I, and hopefully you too, Chris, would be willing to stay overnight in their house to allow them to get away for a short break. Ideally, they would be away from Tuesday until Thursday of next week.'

Chris was immediately enthusiastic.

'What a great idea, Rolf; certainly I'm with you; we must confirm it with the Colbeys right away. Do you mind if I call in and see them when we leave here?'

'Please do,' said Rolf, 'As you know, I'm due to go riding at three o'clock.'

'Do you mind if I come with you?' asked Daphne.

Rolf positively beamed; 'Nothing could please me more.'

'Then I'll hurry along home and get myself ready,' she said with a winning smile, 'and I'll see you at three o'clock.'

When Daphne had gone, Chris said, 'If you don't mind, Rolf, I'm going to suggest to Roger Colbey that while we are at his place, we take a metal detector and make a survey on his behalf; after all, if there is anything to be found it's only right that he should have the benefit of it.'

'Yes, of course, Chris,' Rolf laughed, 'and who knows, we might discover the chest.'

'Do you know,' Chris replied, 'I hadn't even thought of that, but it does put a different light on the matter. In the event of our finding it, had you thought what you would do about it?'

Rolf paused for a few moments and said, 'Honestly, no: it's never been more than a dream. I suppose whoever owns the land that it's found on will have first claim, or perhaps there is an obligation to turn it over to the state, or again, it might rightly belong to Prince Munster's descendants.'

'We ought to make inquiries about the legal situation,' Chris said, but Rolf observed, 'We have a saying in Germany: First we catch the hare, and then we decide how we shall cook it.' He added, 'We don't know what we shall find in the chest when, or if, we ever find it.'

By a gentle pressure on Chris's arm, Kitty reminded him that time was getting on and, looking at his watch, he said, 'We ought to be moving Rolf. Enjoy your ride, and don't let Daphne bully you into going too far. I'll make arrangements with the Colbeys and let you know what's happening.'

Rolf went up to his room and changed into his riding kit. Before leaving the inn he called in on the Broxons to tell them how much they'd all enjoyed the meal. Charles Broxon walked out to the car park with him and held him back for a few minutes.

'Rolf,' he said, 'I couldn't help overhearing something of what you were saying. As an innkeeper, I often overhear things I'm not meant to hear, and as a matter of policy I usually keep them to myself, but when I heard you mention holes being dug in The Park, it reminded me of something I overheard on Wednesday evening.'

'You may remember there were three men sitting over in the corner of the bar. Peter Frobisher had been talking to them, and after he left the men seemed to be quarrelling amongst themselves, so I went over to quieten them. I heard one of them say, 'Let him dig his own b ... holes'. I didn't take too much notice of what their argument was about, but I had to ask them to either tone it down or leave the premises. They left.'

Rolf thanked Charles for the information. It might come in useful he thought, and stored it at the back of his mind.

17

Rolf was feeling quite pleased with himself as he drove into the stable yard. Not only was he going to enjoy an afternoon's riding, he was also going to be with Daphne. She was already mounted when he arrived, and Rupert was saddled and waiting for him. They made a striking picture as they rode side by side along the narrow lane leading towards the open heathland on the edge of the Ashdown Forest.

From being quite young, Daphne had thought there could never be anyone to hold a candle to her brother when it came to horse riding, but as she glanced towards Rolf a strange feeling came over her and she became hopelessly confused. Certainly this man was handsome; he was kind, he was courteous, he was brave. She could have lost her heart completely, but such a thing would be foolish. With an effort, she composed herself and reverted to the role of riding companion whose duty it was to ensure that the charming young foreign visitor should be shown as much as possible of the beautiful English countryside, without being embarrassed by the unwelcome overtures of an immature, lovesick slip of a girl. She would use her head and keep her feelings under control.

Rolf was proud to be riding at her side; she looked more beautiful than ever in her smart riding habit. The black riding cap and jacket made a striking contrast with the white cravat at her throat, and her glorious pale golden hair framing cheeks of pale peach, and eyes of kingfisher blue made her truly delectable. He just could not resist the temptation to steal admiring glances. Occasionally they would urge their mounts into a gallop, when Daphne's hair would flow freely over her shoulders, causing a flutter in the heart of her companion.

They had ridden about five miles when Rolf suggested they should give the horses a short rest; they dismounted by a shallow trout stream, bordered by a copse of sycamores. Rolf tethered the horses to a low overhanging branch of a tree; Daphne lay down on the mossy bank and closed her eyes. Removing her cap, she allowed the gentle breeze to caress her cheeks. She was blissfully happy, and soon she fell into a light sleep in which she dreamed of things which she could never dare to hope. Rolf lay just a few feet away from her with his head cupped in his hands, looking towards her. He would dearly have loved to have leaned over to take her in his arms and proclaim his undying devotion, but instead he lay there dreamily imagining how it would be if only he had the right to love her. He had to keep reminding himself that they knew so little about each other, that he was a foreigner, that maybe she had a boyfriend, or a hundred other reasons she might have for not being interested in him. He had no intention of harming his relationship with her or her family.

They remained there in perfect silence for perhaps half an hour until Daphne roused herself. The horses were beginning to get restless, and so they remounted and pointed them in the direction of home. Few words were spoken, and these were limited to Daphne's efforts to point out landmarks and places of interest.

Chris had already returned home, and he met them in the stable yard. He called out to one of the stable hands to see to the unsaddling of the horses, and Daphne, with a brief murmur of thanks to Rolf, disappeared in the direction of the house. Chris could see the look of disappointment on Rolf's face, but he was too wordly-wise to make any comment; instead, he began to fill him in on the talk he had had with Roger and Beryl Colbey. They were, he told Rolf, very grateful to them for offering to look after their home for two nights next week. He added, 'Mrs Colbey is going to prepare a couple of rooms so that we can sleep there, and she wants us to have the complete run of the place. Roger was highly amused when I suggested that we should use a metal detector to find out what these villains are up to. He said we can dig as many holes as we like provided we fill them in again, and we steer clear of any cultivated areas.'

Rolf told Chris what he had heard from Charles Broxon.

'Perhaps its time we checked on the names old Mr Bell gave us,' Chris said. 'Now what's the best way to go about it? I suppose the easiest way is to refer to the parish registers. You've already made a hit with the rector. Why don't you see what he can do for us?'

'I'll get in touch with Mr Truscott,' Rolf said, 'and I'll also have a word with Martin.'

'Kitty and I are playing tennis down at Eastbourne this evening. Do you play?' Chris asked Rolf.

'A little,' he replied, 'but I'm very much out of practice.'

'Would you care to play?' Chris persisted; 'I'm sure Daphne would like a game, and Kitty prefers doubles. Just wait a moment and I'll pop in the house and ask Daphne if she's able to join us. Oh I trust you've no objections.'

'I should enjoy it very much, but only if Daphne would really like to play; I don't want to upset any plans she might have of her own.'

'Between us,' Chris said, 'we're managing to make it sound terribly complicated, and I'm sure it doesn't have to be. Now just you leave it to me.'

Chris went into the house, leaving Rolf waiting in the car. Ten minutes later he came out accompanied by Daphne who said, 'Rolf, I've made tea; please come in. I'd no idea you were thinking of going yet, and Mummy would be disappointed if you went without saying hello.'

Rolf climbed out of the car and accompanied them indoors, where Mrs Charnford was already pouring out tea. Arthur Charnford was sitting at the table, but he rose to shake hands with Rolf and said, 'I thought Chris was going to keep you out there all day. How did the ride go?'

'It was wonderful,' Rolf said. 'The countryside is so beautiful; ideal for riding. Daphne showed me some delightful places on the forest.'

'I don't suppose you saw any deer; they tend to keep well hidden in the shade during the hot weather. During the autumn and winter months they're much easier to see, and when the weather gets very bad, they often come down to the outskirts of the village foraging for food from the gardens.'

Arthur would have carried on talking about the forest and its wild life for a long time, but his son interrupted to remind them that if they were going to play tennis they ought to be moving.

'I arranged to pick Kitty up at six o'clock,' Chris said, 'so we ought to be down at Eastbourne by half past. I've booked a court for quarter to seven; that should give us comfortable time to change. Shall we call for you, Rolf, on our way to Kitty's? And, by the way, do you have a tennis racket with you?'

'No, I don't have one with me; I hadn't anticipated the possibility of playing. In fact, I have no sports shoes with me either.'

'I'm sure we can kit you out,' Chris said. 'We are roughly the same size, and we'll be able to borrow a racket from Kitty's people.'

Raymond Glover was pleased to be able to supply a racket for Rolf to use; but he was disappointed the young people were not able to call in the house before going for their game. To compensate for this, Mrs Glover asked Kitty to invite them all back for supper at Holmwood.

By the time they had begun to play tennis, the sun, which had been shining brilliantly all day, was beginning to lose some of its power, and was cooling down sufficiently to provide ideal playing conditions. Chris partnered Kitty; they were an ideal combination for mixed doubles. Rolf was decidedly rusty, but as the game progressed he improved considerably. Daphne was at her peak and turned in a brilliant performance which adequately compensated for her partner's lack of practice. The first set was won by Chris and Kitty, the second by Daphne and Rolf. They had time for only one further set and this was won by Daphne and her young German partner.

They returned to Holmwood in excellent spirits, and were met at the door by Kitty's father. Chris introduced Rolf to him and was pleased to see that they were instantly at ease in each other's company.

'I'm very pleased to meet you, sir,' Rolf said, 'and I should like to tell you how much I appreciate your very great kindness in letting me see the plans and photographs of The Park.'

'Not at all, Mr Muller; I was only too pleased to be able to do something towards redeeming the situation. I'm arranging to get the photographs copied so that you can take them home with you to show to your family. It must have been quite a blow to you to see The Park all carved up.'

'I'm sure it's much better this way,' Rolf replied, 'but your photographs have given me a very good idea of what it was once like.'

Connie Glover came over to where the men were standing and shook Rolf warmly by the hand.

'It's lovely to see you again, Mr Muller. Raymond, don't keep them standing there. Hello, Daphne; hello, Chris. Make yourselves comfortable and then we'll eat.'

When they had taken their seats, Kitty assisted her mother by pouring out cups of tea, and Daphne made herself useful by passing sandwiches round. It was clear that Daphne was very much at home with the Glover family.

Over supper, Chris suggested to Rolf that he might care to tell Raymond about the latest developments in The Park saga. They all listened intently as Rolf related details of his visit to the Colbeys, the discovery of the holes, and of the suspicions he harboured as a result of what Chris had seen at Piltdown, as well as what Charles Broxon had overheard at The Chequers.

'Mr and Mrs Colbey are going to London next week,' Rolf said, 'and Chris and I are to spend two nights at their home.'

Chris joined in, 'We may do a bit of digging ourselves while we're there. Roger Colbey is curious to know what is at the back of all the activity, and so we're going to run a metal detector over the part of his ground where the trees are.'

'What will you do Chris, if the diggers turn up when you are there?' Kitty wanted to know.

Chris laughed and said, 'We'll wait until the hole is big enough for them to get inside, and then we'll drop a strawberry net over them,' and then in a more serious vein, 'we're not looking for trouble, are we Rolf?'

'No,' said Rolf, 'we hope to get on with our own digging without interruption. Tomorrow I hope to get a little assistance from the rector; I want to take a look at the parish registers.'

Daphne interrupted. 'How can the parish registers help you, Rolf?'

Chris relieved Rolf of any obligation to explain his motives by saying, 'Be patient my pet, and in due course all will be revealed.'

Mrs Glover tactfully changed the conversation by saying, 'We were delighted to hear of what you're proposing to do for Grace Bell. When do you actually go, Rolf?'

'We shall be leaving on the 2nd September,' Rolf answered. 'It will be rather a long overland drive, but I feel quite sure Mrs Bell will find it well worth the effort. I'm hoping Daphne will be able to share a little of the driving so that we shall be able to arrive on the same day.'

'Perhaps, Rolf, I ought to get in some practice in driving your car,' Daphne said.

'Ever the opportunist,' murmured Chris.

'You beast!' Daphne retorted. 'I hope you don't think that of me, Rolf.'

'No Daphne, I don't; and neither does Chris. I'm more pleased than I can tell you that you are coming with us; and Mrs Bell is very happy with the arrangements.'

'How far is your home from Hamburg?' Raymond Glover asked.

'About thirty miles,' Rolf replied. 'Do you know Hamburg?'

'Yes, I was stationed in Altona for about nine months, back in 1946. I was a very young officer in the Royal Engineers, and we were kept very busy clearing up the bomb damage and restoring the docks; I have some very happy memories of Hamburg. During my off-duty time I would stroll with my fellow officers in the Pflantzen und Blumen Park, or sit on a Sunday afternoon by the Alster and watch the pleasure boats go drifting by. In the evenings we would dine at *The Atlantic Hotel* which for a time was used as an officers' club.'

'Have you returned to Hamburg at all Mr Glover?' Rolf asked.

'I'm afraid not, although I've been several times to other parts of Germany,' Raymond replied.

After supper Daphne said, 'I think I ought to be getting home.'

'Do you want to take my car?' Chris asked her.

'No, I'll walk, thank you,' she said.

Seizing his opportunity, Rolf said, 'I'll be going too. Do you mind if I walk with you, Daphne?'

'Thank you, Rolf; that's very sweet of you,' she replied.

Mrs Glover said, 'If you're not otherwise engaged, why don't you all come and have lunch on Sunday?'

Kitty looked at Chris, and he nodded agreement; Rolf thanked Connie and said he'd be pleased to accept. Only Daphne was slow to respond, but eventually she said, 'If you're sure it won't mean too much extra work for you, Mrs Glover, I'd like to very much.'

'It will be no trouble,' Connie assured her. 'Shall we say one o'clock?'

As soon as they left Holmwood, Daphne adopted a light-hearted air; she hummed various little tunes as they entered her head and every now and then she would say, 'I feel so happy.' Each time she said it, Rolf would ask her why, but she was reluctant to say anything except, 'Why shouldn't I be happy? Perhaps it's because you're taking me to Germany.'

Rolf would have appreciated a little serious conversation, but he was afforded no opportunity. Daphne did however agree when he said, 'Would you come for a little driving experience in the Mercedes tomorrow?'

'Oh, yes please; what time shall I be ready?'

'Can I telephone you?' Rolf said. 'I'm hoping to persuade the rector to spare me a little time in the morning.'

18

On the Saturday morning, Rolf woke and breakfasted early. At nine o'clock he attempted to telephone the rector, but without success. Realising the possibility of the rector's telephone being out of order, he decided to take a walk along to the rectory to see if this was the case. Here again he was out of luck, there was no reply to his ring on the door bell, so he retraced his footsteps. As he was passing the lodge at the entrance to The Park, it occurred to him that Mr Truscott could quite possibly be in the church.

He crossed the road and made his way down the path between two rows of neatly trimmed yew trees. As he entered the porch, the organ was being played, and as he opened the door, he was aware of the unusually fine quality of the music. At first the notes were played softly, and then they increased in volume to a great crescendo, as if the heavens themselves would open. Rolf knelt reverently down in a pew at the rear of the church, his eyes closed in silent prayer. The music went soft again as the organist became aware of his presence in the church.

Rolf rose to his feet and slowly walked towards the chancel steps. As he approached, the organist rose from his seat.

'Please go on playing, sir' Rolf said. 'It was very beautiful.'

'I'd like to,' the organist said, 'but I'm afraid I've stayed too long already, but I do thank you for your appreciation.'

Rolf said, 'I was hoping to find the rector here; I've already called at his home, but he was not there.'

'He'll be away all day I'm afraid,' the organist said, 'He called in here about an hour ago and said he was going up to London. I'll tell you what though; if you want to be sure of seeing him, and if you would seriously like to hear some more of my playing, why not come to the service here tomorrow morning?'

As he spoke the old man had a twinkle in his eye which Rolf could hardly resist.

'I shall do as you suggest,' said Rolf as he stretched out his hand. 'By the way, my name is Rolf Muller.'

'Yes, I know,' the organist said. 'I am Albert Stanford.'

Rolf crossed the road and returned to The Chequers from where he phoned Daphne. She was pleasantly surprised to hear from him quite so early.

'I can be ready in an hour,' she told him. 'If you'd like to call round about half past ten I'll have a coffee ready for you.'

Chris was already out riding on the forest when Rolf arrived at the Charnford's. Arthur was walking towards the house as the Mercedes pulled up by the front door.

'Hello, Rolf,' he called out. 'I'm glad to see you; come along inside and let's have a little talk.'

'Thank you, Mr Charnford; Daphne's expecting me, but I'm a little early,' Rolf said.

'Hello, Daddy,' Daphne said as the two men walked into the house, 'I'll get an extra cup. Look after Rolf for me while I attend to one or two little jobs. I hope you don't mind waiting, Rolf; I'll be about another twenty minutes.'

'No, Daphne,' Rolf replied, 'whenever you're ready will be fine.'

When Daphne left them, her father said to Rolf, 'Chris gave me one or two names he said you were interested in; one was old Eli Parkin from Nutley. I know his son Harry; he's retired now, of course, but he used to be a plumber. He married a girl from Fairwarp, Nellie Bush. They have one daughter, Vera who lives at Three Bridges near Crawley; her married name is Wilkie. I don't know much about him, except that he has a reputation for not being fond of work. They lived in Maresfield for a time, and he did some casual gardening work.'

'That is very useful information, Mr Charnford. Thank you. This morning I called at the rectory to see if Mr Truscott could help me, but unfortunately he will be away all day.'

Daphne came to join them and gave them fresh coffee. She looked ravishing, and Rolf found it difficult to take his eyes off her.

'Rolf and I are going out together, Daddy, so that I can get some practice at driving his car.' Turning to Rolf she said, 'I don't suppose you've any idea how long we shall be gone, Rolf?'

'No,' he said, 'but we may as well make a day of it, if that is agreeable to you.'

'Oh yes, of course; very agreeable. Will you tell Mummy I'll be out for the rest of the day?' she asked her father, and then she added, 'she won't be long; she's gone down to see Mrs Bell.'

Rolf drove as far as Brighton where he had his first sight of the Royal Pavilion. He was captivated with its oriental splendour, and he brought the car to a halt, wanting there and then to take a walk so as to get a closer view. Daphne had to tell him that parking just there was not allowed, and so they drove round to the other side of the floral gardens until they found a free parking meter. They walked through the Pavilion gardens so as to view the building from all angles, and then Daphne suggested a walk through The Lanes which, she said, was an absolute must for visitors to Brighton. Rolf was intrigued at the number of antique shops, coffee houses, small inns and cafés crowded together, and thronged by a cosmopolitan crowd of sightseers.

When they eventually returned to the car, Rolf handed the keys to Daphne, suggesting that she should drive.

'Oh,' she protested, don't you think it would be better if I waited until we're out on the open road before taking over?'

'No, Daphne,' he replied, 'it's better that you get used to driving a strange car in traffic conditions. Anyone can drive a car on a straight road, but you are not just anyone. I wouldn't ask you to drive my car if I was not absolutely confident in you.'

Daphne took the driving seat and immediately felt at ease. Taking the A27 road through Shoreham, alongside the imposing stucture of Lancing College standing high on its hill, they came to a broad stretch of open road where Daphne was able to put her foot down more firmly on the accelerator pedal. She was thrilled by the way the car responded as it gradually increased its speed. The sweet purring of the engine so finely tuned, added to the sense of exhilaration she was experiencing. In a very short time the bridge over the River Arun came in sight, and just beyond, dominating the skyline, the proud towers of Arundel Castle, seat of the Duke of Norfolk, hereditary Earl Marshal of England. They parked the Mercedes alongside the river and walked into the town.

The main street was on a steep hill with a host of antique shops and cafes on either side. At the top of the hill they came to a small inn, white walled, and with small paned windows. It looked very old, but clean and inviting.

'Perhaps we could have lunch here,' Rolf said. Daphne agreed and they went inside. They were shown to an alcove seat where they each took an aperitif, and later to a table covered by a spotless white table cloth.

The choice of food was very comprehensive, and they spent a leisurely ten minutes deciding what they would eat. Prawn cocktails were followed by a fresh salmon salad enhanced by a choice Chablis. The presentation and service, although in less pretentious surroundings, was the equivalent of any Mayfair establishment.

At times their conversation became stilted as they strove valiantly to keep their emotions under control. Neither of them was willing to risk taking a step which could mar their relationship; yet they greatly delighted in each other's company. They were oblivious of other people around them, totally unaware of the admiring glances which from time to time they attracted from members of both sexes.

They were reluctant to leave, and stayed on long after they had finished their meal. Eventually they became aware of the proprietor hovering in the background, and looked round to see there were no other people there. The man came over and asked,

'Is there anything more I can do for you, sir?'

Daphne blushed, and Rolf looking embarrassed said, 'May we have our bill, please?'

'I trust you enjoyed your meal,' the proprietor said.

'It was wonderful' Daphne murmured.

'Excellent,' Rolf added.

He was presented with the bill and settled it with notes from his wallet, adding a generous tip which the proprietor declined, pointing out that a service charge had already been added. As he opened the door for the young couple, he thanked them for their patronage and expressed the hope that he might have the pleasure of serving them again.

They retraced their footsteps down the steep high street until they came to the river. There were several young couples similar to themselves strolling along the banks of the river, and they fell in and walked for half a mile or so along the footpath among the trees, and on to the open meadowland. On their way back to the car, they watched a cricket match. This was something quite new to Rolf and he was fascinated by it. Daphne did her best to explain what it was all about, and they watched for half an hour until it became apparent to Rolf that she was becoming bored. He apologised and suggested that perhaps they should resume their drive.

'Shall I take the wheel, or will you?' he asked.

'I'll drive, Rolf, if you're sure you don't mind,' she answered.

Instead of rejoining the A27 road, they took the A284 until it joined the major A29. They stayed on the A29 only for a short time, leaving it for a minor road which took them through a series of beautiful villages: Storrington, Wiston, Steyning and Poynings, until they eventually reached the enchanting little hamlet of Fulking nestling under the South Downs. There Daphne brought the car to a halt at the side of a small babbling brook.

'Shall we take another short walk, Rolf?' Daphne suggested, 'There is a footpath which leads up on to the Downs, and then perhaps we can call on our way back at a little teashop just along the road from here.'

It was a strenuous walk, taking them over stiles and pebble strewn footpaths which eventually petered out, and climbing up sheep tracks until they were occasionally on all fours. But they were both splendidly fit and enjoyed the unusual exercise. When they arrived at the summit of the hill, they could see for miles in all directions. Daphne delighted in pointing out the many landmarks, places she had often visited in her childhood. They sat down on the warm, dry grass, breathing the invigorating air and, in relative silence, enjoying each other's company.

Their undignified downhill scramble took them only half the time it had taken for the ascent. With glowing cheeks they walked into the tiny shop which doubled for sub-post-office and tea room, a most unlikely looking place for an afternoon tea. They were pleasantly surprised however when they were served with a Sussex cream tea and home-made cakes. Whether it was the high quality of the food or the appetite their hill walking had given them, they could not be sure, but they thoroughly enjoyed what they had.

It was six o'clock when they returned to the car; Rolf took over the driving and Daphne was quite content just to lie back and pleasantly relax.

They arrived home just as Chris was preparing to leave; he got out of his car and came over to them.

'Had a good day?' he asked them. They assured him that they had.

'What do you think of the Mercedes?' he asked Daphne. 'Or didn't you drive after all?'

'Yes, I drove,' she replied, 'and I think she's a dream.'

Chris turned to Rolf and said, 'Sorry, but I must be off; Kitty's expecting me at seven. I'll see you tomorrow at Holmwood then.'

'Oh, yes,' Rolf replied, 'One o'clock for lunch. Auf wiedersehen.'

'You can't go yet, Rolf,' Daphne said as he turned towards the car. 'Come along in, unless you have other plans.' He obediently followed her into the house.

'Hello,' Mrs Charnford greeted them. 'Have you eaten?'

'We've done nothing else all day, Mummy,' Daphne replied, 'but a coffee would be very acceptable.'

'What about you, Rolf?' Sylvia asked the young man.

'Thank you, I couldn't eat anything just now, but a

coffee would be fine.'

'Then you must have something later on,' she insisted, 'if you're not going out again.'

Rolf looked towards Daphne for guidance before he said, 'Er, no I hadn't thought of going anywhere.'

'Before we think of doing anything, we both need to freshen up,' Daphne said.

Rolf was shown to a bathroom by Arthur Charnford, and Daphne went up to her room. Rolf was first to return, feeling and looking refreshed and ready to fall in with whatever Daphne decided she would like to do.

Daphne came down casually dressed which indicated that she was not expecting to go far from home. Mrs Charnford spoke to her husband and said,

'Arthur, why don't you open a bottle of malmsey?' and to her daughter, 'Daphne dear, would you get some glasses, please.'

Daphne looked quizzically at Rolf before complying, and he smiled and nodded agreement, just content to be with her whatever she might do.

The wines of Madeira were new to Rolf, and he was agreeably surprised by the bouquet of the malmsey. It was very different from any of the German wines, and he could think of no French wines he had ever had that could compare with it. It was so smooth to the palate and quite mellowing to the senses. When they first sat down, Daphne and Rolf were sitting at opposite ends of the settee, but after the second glass they were much closer together. Halfway through the third glass, and without even realising it, they were holding hands.

As the evening wore on, Sylvia Charnford said, 'I'll go and get the supper ready. Would you care to lend a hand, Arthur?' Her husband dutifully followed her into the kitchen, leaving the young couple to drink their malmsey at leisure, but the remainder of the wine went untouched. Quite unintentionally, Daphne's head lodged itself against Rolf's shoulder, and half-heartedly she said, 'Oh, I'm sorry,' and slowly began to remove herself, but Rolf put up a hand to stop it happening. They looked into each other's eyes, making no attempt at resistance. Inevitably their lips touched gently at first, but then more firmly. The sound of a discreet cough brought them back to reality.

A coffee-table was drawn up in front of them and was soon laden with a variety of cold meats and salads. Rolf was still feeling replete from all he had eaten earlier in the day, but the food now set before him was so very tempting, and he always had a healthy appetite. He allowed Daphne to fill his plate and it was no problem for him to empty it, and even to accept a second helping when it was offered.

After supper Arthur accompanied his wife once more into the kitchen. While they were attending to the various chores, he observed, 'Those two certainly seem to be getting on well together. I wonder just how deep it goes. I don't want to see either of them get hurt.'

'Don't concern yourself, dear,' Mrs Charnford said, 'they are two very level-headed young people and I'm sure they know their own minds. Daphne has never been one for flirting around, and Rolf is far too decent a fellow to want to string her along.'

Any further discussion was cut short when Daphne came into the kitchen to let them know that Rolf was about to leave. They returned to the drawing-room to wish him goodnight, and he shook hands and thanked them for a very pleasant evening. Daphne accompanied him to his car, and when he was in the driving seat she climbed in beside him. Rolf drew her closely to him, and she responded by putting out her arms to be embraced. The wine they had been drinking was doing for them in one short evening what months of conventional companionship could never have achieved.

It took a long time to say goodnight, and it was the approach of car headlights that caused them eventually to disentangle themselves. Daphne realised that it was Chris's car and, having no mind to be teased by her brother, she offered her lips for a short and tender goodnight kiss and made off indoors. Chris drew up alongside Rolf, and they both got out of their cars.

'Rolf, I didn't expect to see you again quite so soon,' Chris said.

'Your mother invited me to stay for supper,' Rolf explained, 'and we all spent a very pleasant evening together.'

With a little grin, Chris said, 'I'll bet Dad brought the malmsey out.'

'Yes, he did,' Rolf said, 'it was delicious.'

'I hope it didn't cause you to do or say anything you're going to regret tomorrow,' Chris chuckled. He paused, suddenly aware that he had made a bad joke.

Rolf spoke very softly, and very seriously, 'Anything I said or did this evening can only be regretted by me if it has caused distress to anyone else.'

Chris wisely said nothing more on the subject, as he had no wish to hurt his friend.

'And what about you, Chris? Have you done anything special this evening?' Rolf asked.

'We had dinner at The Rose Garden, and then we motored as far as Beachy Head and watched the sun setting over the sea. It was a perfect evening. I'm just beginning to realise what I've been missing all these years.'

Rolf understood what Chris was experiencing. Those two men had so much in common.

19

On Sunday morning Rolf looked out of his window at The Chequers and watched the people making their way down the yew lined pathway to the morning service at the parish church. One or two cars were drawn up in the car park, but for the most part the worshippers arrived on foot. At first, Rolf was hesitant about joining them. He had not been in the habit of church going and had seldom been since his childhood days other than at Easter and Christmas, and the occasional wedding or funeral.

Eventually he found himself walking resolutely across the road and before he knew it, Martin Bell was showing him to a pew. It was almost as if Albert Stanford had waited for the young man to arrive before starting his morning voluntary. Rolf had scarcely taken his seat when he began to play. 'Jesu, Joy of Man's Desiring' was the tune he had selected. He was putting his whole heart into his playing, and every ear in the church was tuned to the melody. He was so absorbed in his performance, that he failed to notice his cue when the rector took his place at the chancel steps. The congregation could scarcely refrain from giving a round of applause as his short recital came to a close.

The Reverend Percival Truscott, resplendent in surplice of pure white, led his flock in prayer, exhorting them to confess to Almighty God their manifold sins and wickednesses. When the first hymn was announced, and Albert Stanford played the first few lines of introduction, it seemed that it was going to be a stirring hymn. But alas, no; either the hymn was not a particularly well-known one, or the people were reluctant to create discord by their inability to match the sounds of the organ with their own inadequate vocal talents.

Mrs Truscott was the sole occupant of the front pew; it was traditionally reserved for members of the rector's family. The present incumbent having married rather late in life, had not been blessed with progeny, and so Amelia was left to stand, or sit, alone.

In the third row were the Misses Prudence and Verity Smythe, a position they had occupied on and off since infancy, when a governess had been charged with the responsibility of attending them and their numerous brothers and sisters now departed. Prudence, the elder of the two, had never married, her life having been devoted to the service of others. She had served in two world wars as a Red Cross nurse. She was well-known and greatly respected throughout the village and surrounding countryside as a friend of the poor and needy. Verity in her youth had been the tomboy of the family and now, even in her seventieth year, she retained a roguish twinkle in her eye. Her married name was Lady Crampton, but she had been widowed for almost ten years, and on the death of her husband she had reverted to her maiden name and returned to the family home on the edge of Ashdown Forest. Here she would live out the rest of her days alongside her elder sister Prudence.

Martin Bell was sharing the duty of sidesman with the elderly churchwarden Ralph Milburn. Old Ralph was very conscious of his position in the church. Over many years he had managed to repel a host of would-be worshippers in his efforts to maintain the status quo; he cared little for new fangled-ideas. The 1662 prayer book had been good enough for his father and grandfather before him, and no parson with modern ideas would be permitted to introduce alternative services as long as he lived.

Roger and Beryl Colbey, arriving amongst the late-comers, saw Rolf sitting alone and went to join him. Mr Turley the grocer turned round in his seat and accorded Rolf a broad smile and nod of recognition. His wife Edith bravely resisted the temptation to look round for a glimpse of the young man about whom she had heard so much but so far had not seen.

Peter and Doris Frobisher were sitting just behind the

Turleys. From time to time Doris would cast an eye over the congregation, carefully ignoring the lesser order of villagers, but at the same time ensuring that she caught the eye of those who in her opinion were people of consequence. She wondered if Lady Grantwell might be in church this morning, although one could hardly expect it, in view of the rector's disgraceful behaviour in denying her ladyship the pleasure of opening the church fête.

The first lesson was read audibly and clearly by Commander Oswald Brewster RN retired. He was distinctly proud of his ability to command the attention of all the congregation; all that is, with but one exception, and that one was his own small grandson. Master Horace Potter, five year old son of Emily Potter (née Brewster) was unused to the rigours of wooden seating, and was not averse to letting it be known that he was both bored and uncomfortable. Furthermore, he felt it incumbent on himself to turn round at frequent intervals and display the greater part of his tongue for the benefit of anyone who happened to be unfortunate enough to be in his line of vision. Grandpapa would be terribly angry when they returned to the Manor, but until then Horace held the advantage, knowing that the old gentleman through bitter experience, would not risk the humiliation of a show of tantrums in public.

There were very few people in the congregation under the age of fifty, but there were two or three, and this was perfectly evident during the singing of the second hymn, 'The King of Love My Shepherd Is'. From somewhere to the rear of where Rolf was sitting there came the sound of a soprano voice which had not been present during the singing of the first hymn. This voice was so rich and clear with perfect pitch and tone, that it compelled him to glance over his shoulder in an effort to locate its source. Rolf was at once astounded and thrilled when he saw who the singer was; it was Daphne Charnford. She was sitting alongside her mother, who smiled briefly as she noticed his glance which was beginning to develop into a gaze. With an effort, Rolf composed himself and turned his attention to the rector as the hymn drew to a close.

Before commencing his sermon, the rector read out

several notices concerning the activities for the week ahead, the most prominent of which was the annual church fte on Saturday, to be opened by Herr Doktor Rolf Muller. He hoped they would all come along to support the worthy cause.

The sermon was not one of the Reverend Percival's better efforts, but even if it had been, it would have been wasted on the young German. Rolf was unable to concentrate. He had never been in love before and here he was, completely and utterly enthralled, unable to take part in any of the things going on around him. It seemed his heart was ready to burst; he knew he was in love with Daphne; he had never in his whole life been so sure of anything. But did she feel the same about him? Dare he build up his hopes? Did he have the right to expect Daphne to care for him. He began to reason with himself, and came to the conclusion that he had no right; he could expect nothing. Hope gave way to despair; he dare not risk a second glance.

Another hymn was announced, and Rolf suddenly realised that the sermon had come to an end. The sidesmen moved slowly among the congregation taking up the offering. When Martin Bell drew alongside Rolf he whispered softly, 'Can you wait for me after the service is over?' Rolf nodded and turned his attention to the hymn. Again he heard only one voice; not that Daphne was deliberately singing above the other voices. It was not in her nature to try to be conspicuous, but had there been another hundred voices, he would have noticed no other.

There was a short time of prayer, and then followed the closing hymn. As he turned to leave his pew Rolf was besieged by a number of people headed by George Turley, who felt it to be his duty to introduce the young gentleman; firstly to his wife Edith, and then to anyone within hailing distance. Rolf accepted the situation graciously, showing no sign of his annoyance. Much to Rolf's distress, the Colbeys were denied the opportunity of a word, and made their way to the door. Prudence and Verity Smythe were delighted to meet him; Prudence pressed a calling card into his hand and said, 'We should be pleased if you would call on us some time, Dr Muller.'

By the time Rolf had escaped, Daphne and her mother were nowhere in sight. At the church door he shook hands with the rector and forgot completely that he had a request to make of him. He waited outside the church until Martin came out, and invited him to accompany him to The Chequers. The bar was crowded, and so Rolf ordered two lagers which they took up to his room. They were both pressed for time, and so Martin came straight to the point.

'I called in here last night and I saw young Pattaway; he was very much the worse for drink. He said he was hoping to see you as he wanted to give you a warning. It seems that a Miles Ritchie, brother of one of the villains who attacked Nancy, is hanging around the village. He's out to avenge his brother, but the guv'nor, whoever he is, is planning something big, and has told him to hold his horses for a few more days. Young Alan has been instructed to carry on shadowing you and to report back with any information he can pick up. At the moment he says he's in bad books because he hasn't come up with anything useful.' Rolf was sorry he had to cut the meeting short, but before they parted he asked after Mrs Bell. He was assured that she was in good spirits and was now keenly anticipating her visit to Germany.

Chris and Daphne were already at Holmwood by the time Rolf arrived. Kitty met him at the door with a smile of welcome and led him in to where the others were sipping sherry. Her father shook him by the hand and invited him to take a glass. Connie Glover joined in the welcome to which Rolf replied in his usual charming manner. His main concern, however, was to see how Daphne would receive him. She shook hands with him and said, 'Hello, Rolf. It was quite a surprise seeing you in church this morning. Did you enjoy the service?'

Rolf smiled wryly and replied, 'I enjoyed being there, but I fear I did not benefit much from the rector's sermon.'

'Neither did I,' Daphne said. 'It wasn't particularly uplifting.' Rolf resisted the temptation to tell her he was oblivious to anything else other than the singing of one of the members of the congregation.

Kitty opened up a conversation with Daphne, and this gave Rolf an opportunity to speak to Chris and Raymond.

'I've just been talking to Martin Bell. He called in at The Chequers yesterday evening and he saw our young friend Pattaway who was apparently hoping that one of us would be around. There is a man by the name of Miles Ritchie, brother of one of the men who tussled with me, letting it be known that he intends to do me some mischief. Alan also told Martin that he has been instructed to continue to keep me under surveillance, and to report on any information he can gather. Something significant is being planned to take place within the next few days.'

Chris said, 'We ought to arrange to be at The Chequers tonight when Alan drops in. Perhaps he knows more than he was prepared to tell Martin. In the meantime, Rolf, you'll have to make yourself as inconspicuous as possible.'

Rolf was indignant and said, 'You surely don't imagine that I'm going to hide myself just because some irresponsible hooligan is boasting of what he intends to do to me.'

'Sorry, Rolf,' Chris replied, 'I should have known better; but the situation is rather a tricky one. We don't know what is going to happen, when it will happen, or who is going to make it happen.'

Raymond Glover cut in and said, 'If I might offer some advice . . .'

'Go ahead,' said Chris.

'Well now, let's take the third point first. You know one of the persons involved, and that, from what you have already observed, is surely my near neighbour Peter Frobisher. Let us assume that he is the organiser, and that he is the man who has ordered your young friend Pattaway to glean some information.' The other two nodded their heads in affirmation that they agreed so far.

'If he wants information,' Glover continued, 'then let's jolly well see that he gets information.'

The significance of what Mr Glover was saying struck home, and he asked them, 'Just how well do you know this youth, and how far can he be trusted?' Chris detailed the circumstances of their first encounter with Alan Pattaway and of their promise to help him out of the sorry plight he was in.

Raymond carried on, 'Now it is important that you, or should I say we, take the initiative. We must force our adversary, whoever he is, to play his hand when we are ready, not when it suits him.'

Mrs Glover called them to lunch and they took their places in the dining-room; Rolf was pleased to find himself sitting by Daphne's side. For the time being, serious matters were put to one side, and they set about enjoying a typical English Sunday lunch. Rolf told the others about the invitation he had been given to visit the Misses Smythe, whereupon Kitty and Daphne exchanged glances and then Kitty said, 'Don't disappoint them, Rolf; they'd be awfully hurt if you didn't find time to go.'

Daphne added, 'They're terribly interesting people, Rolf; it would be a sad omission if you were to leave Maresfield without having been to Woodcott. Why don't we all go this afternoon?'

Rolf was alarmed at the idea of calling in force without having given prior warning, but Raymond Glover said, 'Don't worry, Rolf; Connie and I have other things to do, but the Smythes will, I'm sure, be delighted if you drop in on them. They would much prefer it to a formal visit.'

Daphne said, 'Oh, let's do that, Rolf!' and she squeezed his arm as she said it. Prudence is getting quite cross with me because I haven't been for such a long time.'

It was agreed that the four of them should take a walk in the forest and, on the way, they would casually look in at Woodcott. Before they left, Raymond told the other two men that he would put his mind to the task of working out a plan of campaign. There was a glint in his eye, and Chris sensed that he was going to relish the challenge of pitting his wits against Frobisher.

Daphne and Kitty walked on ahead, leaving Chris and Rolf to talk quietly between themselves.

'Unless some specific crime is committed, there's no point in calling in the police,' Chris said. 'They're only interested in solving crime, not preventing it. We don't know how many people we're up against; we must ask Alan if he has any idea, and we shall need to recruit a few dependable chaps. Charles Broxon is the man to handle that part of the problem.'

For the first stage of their walk they kept to the side of the road, and shortly before they reached the turning which would take them towards Woodcott, they were overtaken by an ancient blue Morris Minor. At the wheel was Miss Verity Smythe, and she gave them a friendly smile and waved to them as she passed. Before turning off the main road, she pulled into the side and waited for the young people to reach her.

'Look here,' Miss Verity said, 'why don't you pop in and see us? Prudence will be quite devastated if you're coming this way without calling on us. Daphne, my dear, put some pressure on them, that's my girl.'

Daphne feigned a protest. 'But Miss Verity, there are four of us; don't you think that's rather too many to drop on you unannounced?'

'Nonsense, my child,' she replied, 'you must come.'

Miss Verity drove on ahead and told her sister that the young people were on their way. The four deliberately walked slowly, giving Miss Prudence time to absorb the news that a minor horde would shortly be descending on them. It made no difference, of course; the house was quite untidy, and even had Prudence been expecting them, the same delightful state of chaos would have prevailed. They had help in the house only two days a week, and Mrs Green's time was taken up mostly on chattering and making cups of tea.

Neither of the sisters was in any way domesticated. In their childhood they had been used to a host of servants, and their accomplishments had been academic rather than artisan. There were several paintings on the wall, two of which bore the signatures of old masters. There were four landscapes which Miss Prudence herself had painted in oils. Rolf was full of admiration, and Chris expressed his surprise at the risk the two sisters were taking by having such treasures on view. Miss Prudence said she had no intention of hiding the pictures.

'As far as I'm concerned pictures are to be seen, not hidden away in vaults. We've been burgled three times during the past six months, but none of our paintings have been taken. Several of our most valuable antiques have been stolen and there's not much left now. We've been advised to leave here, but this has been our home for many years, and we're staying!'

'Have the police had any success in tracing the thieves?' Chris asked.

'They have their suspicions, but nothing more,' Prudence replied.

'They're keeping a night-time surveillance on all the properties on the forest, but it's far too big a task for their limited resources. Do you have such problems in Germany, Dr Muller?'

'I'm afraid we do,' Rolf said, 'although it isn't so bad in my part of Germany as it appears to be with you.'

Miss Verity escorted Daphne and Kitty on a tour of the gardens. They had often been there as children and knew every part, but it was a constant delight to see new varieties of flowers and shrubs, and the sisters made frequent additions to their stock. The tennis court had given way to a formal lawn surrounded by a herbaceous border. Miss Verity was proud of this, as also her vegetable patch which kept them and often enough many other Maresfield people, in fresh produce for the greater part of the year.

Miss Prudence took the two men out into the garden to join the others. Chris fell in with the ladies, but Miss Prudence took Rolf to one side. When they were out of earshot she said, 'Is it true that you have some connection with the family of Prince Munster?'

Rolf replied, 'The connection is so remote that it is hardly worth mentioning. My great-grandfather was a second cousin of the prince and they were also very good friends. Everything I know about the Munster family I heard from my grandfather, Karl Muller; he used to come to Maresfield Park as a child.'

The old lady clutched at Rolf's sleeve;

'Did you say Karl Muller was your grandfather?'

'Yes, that is so,' Rolf replied. 'Have I startled you?' Instead of answering she asked, 'Is Karl still living?'

'No,' Rolf answered, 'he died earlier this year. Did you know him?'

'Yes, I knew Karl,' she said slowly, 'my brother Philip and I used to go to The Park to play with the Munster boys during school holidays, and sometimes Karl would also be there. He was a charming boy; you must tell me all about him sometime. Are you staying long in Maresfield?'

'I shall be returning to Germany next week, but perhaps I can call on you again the next time I come to England.'

'Yes, indeed you must,' Prudence replied. 'There are many things I want to ask you. Will it be long before you come again?'

Rolf assured the old lady that he intended to return soon, and regularly. The sisters were disappointed that the young people were unable to stay to take tea with them, but they were appeased when Kitty promised to pay them another visit quite soon. As they walked on, Rolf related to the others what Miss Prudence had told him concerning his grandfather.

'The old gentleman seems to have been very well liked during his time here in Maresfield, Rolf. He really must have been a charming boy,' Daphne said.

'It's wonderful to have good report of the people one loves,' said Rolf, and for the rest of the walk he remained silently contemplative.

They arrived back at Holmwood just as Mrs Glover was preparing tea. Kitty and Daphne disappeared into the kitchen and Chris and Rolf were beckoned into Raymond's study.

'Right,' Raymond said, 'I've been working out a plan of action which should bring matters to a head. I suggest, Rolf, that you write a letter to your father telling him that you have discovered the whereabouts of the chest and are making plans to dig it up on Thursday of this week. Make it a nice, chatty letter and tell him exactly how you intend to carry out the project, detailing the precise location. Explain how you have marked the site, and tell him that only two of you know about it and will be struggling to handle it between you. The letter, clearly addressed to your father, should be left open and put in a conspicuous place in your room. You'll have to arrange with young Pattaway to go into your room and discover it. He will then take it to his car park rendezvous and hand it over to his contact. If his contact is the man I think he is, he will have no difficulty in reading it. Frobisher is an accomplished linguist. No doubt, having read it, he will instruct the youth to replace it, leaving Rolf none the wiser.'

'I get it,' Chris exclaimed. 'Frobisher will rush to have the chest dug up before we do. We lie in wait and catch them in the act.'

'Not so fast, Chris,' Raymond cautioned. 'There's no point in stopping them in their tracks; what good would it do? Supposing we were able to muster sufficient men to overpower them. All we should be able to do would be to hand them over to the police, and what then? They'd be charged with trespassing, and very little else.'

'I see what you mean,' said Chris. 'It would be better if they actually found the chest and attempted to make off with it.'

'Exactly!' Raymond said. 'What we have to do is to ensure that they find a chest and, having found it, we put a tail on them and let them lead us to their clearing house. We shall have to arrange with the police to be ready to move in and take over; how they do it, of course, is a matter for them to work out. They have the experience and we must not attempt to tell them their business.'

'Can you be sure of their co-operation?' Chris asked.

'If my hunch is correct,' said Raymond, 'the people behind this enterprise are the same ones who have been organising the burglaries over the past few months, and the police will take any steps they can to lay hands on them. I know the people at County Police Headquarters; I think you can safely leave it to me to persuade them to co-operate.'

'You don't suppose Frobisher will take it to his own place, do you?' Chris asked.

'I doubt it very much,' Raymond replied, 'and we cannot be at all certain that he is the man at the top.'

'How do we conjure up a chest?' Chris wanted to know.

'A chest is easy; I have two or three very old packing cases at the office,' said Raymond. 'These chaps won't know precisely what it is they are looking for. You can ask

Martin Bell if he has a couple of old padlocks; in any case, we should seek his advice.'

'Where do we make the discovery?' Rolf asked.

'I might have suggested you could do it here,' Raymond replied, 'but that would probably cause suspicion. As the Colbeys are going to be away, why not make it at their place? With their permission, of course.'

'That sounds very sensible to me,' Chris said. 'If you wish, Rolf, I'll go round there when we leave here.'

20

In his room at *The Chequers*, Rolf carefully drafted a letter to his father:

> The Chequers Inn,
> Maresfield,
> Sussex.
> *18 August 1983*

Dear Father,

I write to give you good news.

With the help of my very good friend Chris Charnford, the chest has been found! Grandfather's diary proved to be useful after all, and the five oaks which he mentioned are still there. It was difficult at first to locate them, as only three oaks are standing on the property where the chest was buried, and the other two are separated from them by a boundary wall. The owner of the property, Mr Colbey, is a very kind gentleman, and he agrees that the chest should be opened at our embassy in London.

We are obliged to do everything in absolute secrecy, as other people are also trying to get their hands on it. Chris and I have left the chest in its burial place, and have replaced the soil over it; we are planning to recover it on Thursday of this week after it is dark. The location has been well marked without being too conspicuous to other people; we have tipped an old wheelbarrow over it.

It is going to be very difficult for the two of us to remove it; but it is most important that no one else knows about it. We shall drive overnight to London as soon as I can get it into my car.

I shall be home with you on the third as arranged. Please give my love to Mother and Helga.

> Your loving son,
> Rolf.

Having completed the letter, Rolf placed it on the centre of the dressing-table in his room. At the side of it he put an envelope which was addressed to his father and stamped with the appropriate postage for transmission to Germany. Having done this he was careful to leave his door slightly ajar, and went down the stairs to where Charles Broxon was standing by the reception alcove.

'Are you likely to be around this evening Rolf?' he asked his guest.

'I can't be sure, Charles; a lot depends on other people, but I'll be calling back shortly. By the way, don't be concerned to find my door open; I want it to be left that way for a very good reason which I'll explain another time.'

Rolf left The Chequers and went down to Martin Bell's cottage. Martin welcomed him and led him inside to where Grace, having heard and recognised his voice, was waiting to receive him.

'How nice to see you, Mr Muller. Will you have a cup of tea?'

'Thank you, Mrs Bell, but no,' Rolf said, 'I'm afraid I have only a little time.' He turned to Martin and said, 'I wonder if you can help me. I'm looking for two large padlocks, and Raymond Glover suggested that you might possibly have some old ones.'

'You're very welcome to anything I've got,' Martin told him.

'Perhaps I can find you some fairly new ones; you'd better come through to the garage and I'll see what I've got.'

'I'd rather not have new ones if you don't mind, Martin, I'll tell you why.'

Rolf brought Martin up to date with events. The old man became quite excited and was keen to get involved. Martin didn't have a car, which was just as well as there was no room for one in his garage. Rummaging through his hoard of junk, he eventually found a pair of rusty old padlocks of the required kind; but better than that, he located an old chest that his grandfather had made. It was packed solidly with a variety of iron objects and could not be moved, but Martin said it wouldn't take him long to empty it. Rolf suggested that some of the objects should be left in the chest to give the impression of its being full.

Having explained to Martin about the letter he had written, he enlisted his help, suggesting that he should meet Alan Pattaway in the car park after the evening service, and arrange with him to find the letter. Rolf went on to stress the importance of having the letter handed over to Alan's contact, and this Martin agreed to impress on the youth.

Having returned to The Chequers, Rolf rang through to the Charnfords to advise Chris of what he had managed to accomplish. Daphne answered the phone, and when he asked if he might speak to Chris, she said, 'Oh Rolf, I am disappointed,' and teasingly added, 'I thought you might have wanted to speak to me; I'll get Chris for you.'

Before he had the chance to reply, Chris came to the telephone. 'I've spoken to Roger Colbey,' Chris said, 'and he's given permission for us to mount the operation as planned. I can't say that he was particularly keen on the idea, but he realises the seriousness of the situation and wants to co-operate as best he can. I didn't mention who our prime suspect is.'

Rolf said, 'I've written the letter, and Martin is going to see Alan to brief him; I shall leave the door to my room slightly ajar with the letter in a conspicuous place. I went to see Martin and he has a chest which will be ideal for our purposes; we can collect it tomorrow morning if you are free. Can you let Mr Glover know what we've done?'

'I'll be calling for Kitty shortly, and I'll update him. By the way, my sister's hovering in the background; I'll be in touch.'

Rolf said, 'Perhaps I could have a word with Daphne.'

Daphne came to the phone; she said nothing until Chris had disappeared, and then it was simply, 'Hello, Rolf!' Her voice was not intentionally seductive, but it was soft and gentle; it sent a thrill through the whole of his body.

'May I see you this evening, Daphne?' he asked her.

'If you like.'

When he had regained his composure he said, 'Perhaps we could drive down to Eastbourne and take a walk along the promenade. When can you be ready?'

'I'm ready now,' she replied.

'Then I'll come for you right away.'

Rolf was there within a quarter of an hour; Daphne was waiting by the door, and as soon as the car drew to a halt she got in beside him.

'May I say how perfectly charming you're looking, Daphne?' Rolf said.

'Why, thank you, sir; how perfectly gallant of you to say so,' Daphne replied with playfully feigned coyness.

It was a beautiful summer evening. Holiday makers of all ages thronged the promenade at Eastbourne. There were no vacant seats at the bandstand where a concert was in progress. For a while the two young people lingered to listen to a selection of Sousa marches before continuing their walk.

'I think perhaps we ought to look for somewhere a little less crowded,' Daphne suggested. 'Perhaps Beachy Head would be better than here.'

'Whatever you wish,' Rolf replied.

They returned to the car and drove leisurely along the westerly stretch of the promenade, eventually climbing up the steep winding road leading to the heights overlooking the Beachy Head Lighthouse, and from where they had a marvelous bird's eye view of the town. There were lots of cars parked in the various lay-bys, seemingly deserted, as the owners, mostly young couples, wandered off to find solitude on the Downs.

Having securely locked the doors of the Mercedes, they went off, a happy young couple enjoying each other's company, as if they had not a care in the world. Every now and then the footpath they were following would peter out, and they would have to scramble precariously over the steep, grassy slopes. At such times Daphne would laughingly reach out a hand for Rolf to assist her over the rough terrain. He felt wretched each time they regained the footpath, when he would have to relinquish his hold.

After half an hour or so of strenuous walking, Daphne called for a brief rest. They sat down side by side on a patch of grass warmed by the sun, sheltered on three sides by gorse bushes. The setting sun was spreading a mantle of pure gold over the calm sea below, just as it had been the first time the two of them had walked together, not far from where they now were.

As they relaxed, taking in the evening air, they talked about the things that interested them, and found that they had so much in common.

The lighthearted, coquettishness which Daphne had at times playfully adopted, seemed this evening to have deserted her. As much as she had wanted to have a mild flirtation, this evening she could not bring herself to treat Rolf in this way. He was a very serious person, and she had no mind to hurt him in any way. Suddenly, and without any apparent reason she turned to him and said, 'Come on, Rolf, please take me home.'

It was just after half past seven when The Reverend Percival Truscott brought his evening service to a close. The congregation was not long in dispersing, and the few cars parked across the road were already being driven away when Martin Bell walked slowly up the path leading from the church to the car park. He stood by the lych gate keeping an eye open for the arrival of Alan Pattaway, hoping that he would not be late. He did not have long to wait before the battered old Ford Consul turned into the church car park. Martin walked casually across the road and tapped on the window of the car. Alan wound down the window and recognising Martin Bell, said, 'Wot d' yer want? Nobody's supposed ter know I'm 'ere.'

Martin told him about the letter waiting to be discovered at The Chequers, and advised him to go quickly into Rolf's room and get it to show to his contact. Alan was at first reluctant to comply, but it slowly dawned on him that this might make up for any lack of information he had been hitherto able to supply. He accompanied Martin to the inn, and asked him to keep a lookout as he swiftly mounted the stairs. He had no difficulty in locating the letter, and returned to Martin, patting his pocket to indicate that he had it with him.

Alan returned to his car to find an angry Peter Frobisher waiting for him.

'Just what do you think you're playing at?' demanded Frobisher. 'How dare you keep me waiting.'

The tone of Frobisher's voice indicated that young Alan was meant to cringe, but instead, he looked the man squarely between the eyes and said, 'I bin doin' a reccy, ain't I? Yer said yer wanted information so I bin lookin' fer it.' He pulled the letter from his pocket. 'I found this up in the geezer's room.'

Frobisher snatched the letter from him, avidly reading its contents. Alan watched the changing expression on his face as he read it a second time, and then he made notes before saying, 'Well done, young man; now you must put this back exactly where you got it from. You can do something else for me; I want you to go into The Chequers bar and look out for Miles Ritchie; do you know him?'

'Yes,' said Alan, 'E's the 'eavy bloke from Crawley.'

'Tell him to telephone me urgently,' said Frobisher. 'I'll be waiting by the phone, so tell him not to keep me hanging about.'

Frobisher hurried home and went straight to the telephone. The call he made was answered immediately; with great excitement he gave the news of his dramatic discovery; he was as pleased with himself as any dog wagging his tail and waiting to be patted on the back. He was adequately rewarded by the expression of approval he received. Even the peremptory instruction he was given failed to cool the warm glow of self-satisfaction that enveloped him. The instruction was, 'You will deliver it here, unopened on Tuesday evening after dark.'

He had barely replaced the receiver when his phone bell rang.

'Ah, Ritchie, thank you for ringing straight away. Now listen very carefully; important developments have taken place, and it looks as though we shall need to go into action sooner than I had anticipated. I want you to contact your friends and arrange a meeting for tomorrow evening at eight o'clock; the usual place, King's Standing.'

'What was all that about?' his wife wanted to know.

'The less you know about it at this stage, the better,' Frobisher replied. 'Let's just say that before this week is out we'll be somewhat wealthier than we are now.'

Doris Frobisher knew better than to question her husband too closely about financial matters. She was content to enjoy the fruits of his operations without the inconvenience of a guilty conscience.

21

On Monday morning, Chris called at The Chequers for Rolf and together they drove down to Martin Bell's cottage. Martin had been up quite early and had sorted out the contents of the chest; anything of value had been removed and had been replaced by an assortment of scrap iron. Chris was impressed by what he saw, but he said, 'Martin, we came to give you a hand; it wasn't meant that you should do it all by yourself.'

'It was no trouble,' Martin assured him. 'Are you ready to take it now?'

Chris said, 'We may as well take it out of your way and get it buried before the weather changes. Let's get it into my car boot.' Martin fastened the chest securely, using the two rusty old padlocks. They were extremely difficult to snap closed, and it took all his strength to accomplish the feat.

The three of them struggled to carry the chest and load it into the Jaguar. When they arrived at the Colbeys, Roger was still having breakfast. Beryl met them at the door and insisted that they should have coffee.

'I'm sorry Hopkins won't be here to help you,' Roger said, 'but he's having the week off.'

Rolf smiled and said, 'So much the better, Mr Colbey; we'll manage quite well if we can just borrow the necessary digging tools and a wheelbarrow.'

Mrs Colbey produced coffee and they debated together on the proposed digging operation. Roger agreed on the site for the new hole; just to the right of the three oaks by the boundary fence. Martin said he would need to return home for a couple of hours to see to Grace's needs, and so they decided to begin their task at two o'clock.

They took Martin home, and then Chris and Rolf drove

to the Livery Stables. Arthur Charnford was in the stable
yard, and Chris left Rolf to talk with him while he went
into the house to look for suitable working clothes for the
laborious task ahead. Sylvia Charnford came out to look
for her husband, and seeing Rolf said, 'Good morning,
Rolf; I hope you'll stay and have lunch with us.'   'Thank
you, Mrs Charnford; you're very kind,' he said.

Chris, seeing Daphne at work in the kitchen,
mentioned that Rolf was in the stable yard and would
shortly be coming into the house. She made a sudden
dash up to her room, discarded her pinafore and quickly
made adjustments to her hair and general appearance.

Sylvia Charnford led the men indoors and deftly laid
an extra place at the table. Daphne made no secret of the
fact that she was pleased to see their young visitor and
said to him, 'I was hoping I might see you today, Rolf.'

Her heart missed a beat as he murmured, 'I was sharing
the hope with you.'

Arthur Charnford cut across their thoughts by saying
to Chris and Rolf, 'I hope you chaps know what you're
doing.'

'We do know what we're doing, Father; we only hope
that the police do their stuff. Kitty's father is dealing with
that side of the exercise; he knows the people at Police
Headquarters.'

Daphne spoke up, 'If Mr Glover is arranging it, you've
nothing to worry about.'

'Well said, Daphne,' cried Chris, and added, 'like
daughter, like father.'

Realising the need for the men to have lunch quickly,
Daphne said, 'Will you be coming back here later on
Rolf?'

'Yes, I suppose I shall,' Rolf replied. 'I shall need to
change back into my own clothes, and it is better that I do
it here.'

'Then I'll see you shortly.' With that she left them and
walked out into the garden, leaving them all speculating.

Chris took Rolf up to his room where he kitted him out
in boots, a pair of working corduroys, a pullover and an
old hacking jacket. When he had dressed, Chris
presented him with a tweed cap, so that he looked like a

stable hand. They went downstairs where Mr and Mrs Charnford were waiting to see the transformation. Sylvia held her sides with laughing and her husband joined in.

'All you need now, Rolf, is a piece of straw to put in your mouth.'

Rolf was relieved that Daphne had not waited to see him.

They called to pick up Martin and drove back to The Park, managing to make the short journey without being observed. Roger Colbey was waiting for them, and presented them with a shovel and spades. He said, 'I've left the tool-shed unlocked in case there's anything else you might need. Come back to the house and clean yourselves up when you've finished, and Beryl will make a cup of tea for you. I'm sure you'll be ready for one.'

They selected a place which they felt would be clear of such obstacles as tree roots, and marked out an approximate digging area. An old tarpaulin sheet was brought from the shed and laid on the ground to take the soil. Martin took the first stint, cutting through the dry turf, and making the way clear for the two younger men to attack the subsoil. Neither Chris nor Rolf had experienced this type of work before, but both applied themselves vigorously to the common task.

It was not until they had been digging for two hours that they were satisfied with the hole. They then took the wheelbarrow to the car and lifted the chest from the boot on to it; they wheeled their heavy load over to the hole and carefully lowered the chest from the boot into it. They experienced a certain satisfaction as they tightly rammed down over the chest all the stones and soil, ensuring that the task of exhumation would be at least as difficult as their own task had been. When the work was completed, they turned the wheelbarrow on end as a marker. Returning the tools and the tarpaulin to the shed, the three men then made their way back to the house to advise Roger Colbey that their task had been completed.

'We've left the wheelbarrow on site,' Chris told Mr Colbey. 'It will serve as a marker. We don't want the treasure hunters to lose too much time looking around in the wrong place.' Beryl Colbey brought out a tray with a pot of tea and sandwiches on to the terrace, giving them an excuse to sit down and rest from their labours. There was a brief discussion about things which would require attention during the Colbeys' absence. Roger produced a duplicate set of keys and explained the security system for the house. He gave them the address and telephone number of Beryl's sister in London in case it should be necessary to contact him. Beryl then took over and gave them carte blanche to make use of anything in the larder and refrigerator. She also suggested that perhaps Daphne might be recruited to prepare their meals.

Chris and Rolf managed to get back to the Livery Stables without being noticed by anyone who might be interested in their movements. Again, Rolf was thankful that Daphne was nowhere in sight, and he hurried up to Chris's bedroom to change into his own clothes. As he washed himself, he noticed one or two red marks on his hands. He didn't have to be a doctor to realise that by tomorrow he would have blisters.

Daphne came in from the garden as Rolf was descending the stairs.

'How did it go, Rolf?' she asked.

'There were no problems,' he replied, 'it was quite straightforward.'

'Let me see your hands,' she demanded. He obediently held out his hands, and Daphne took them tenderly in her own.

'Oh, Rolf, you're going to have blisters there.' Her look of concern was so real that Rolf felt almost glad that he would have blisters. He could not resist the temptation to take her in his arms; he drew her closer to himself, and without any conscious movement he found his lips pressing firmly on her mouth. There was no resistance; Daphne responded eagerly.

As Chris came down the stairs, he was softly whistling a tune. Daphne released herself from Rolf's arms and drew him swiftly towards the door leading out onto the lawn. There were things to be said that were not for the ears of others. When they were out of sight and earshot they stopped walking, and as if to confirm that what happened before was real and not a mere flight of fancy, they embraced and kissed, again and again.

'Oh Rolf, my darling I do love you,' Daphne murmured. There was no verbal response from Rolf; no words could have expressed the emotions he was feeling.

When Daphne finally released herself, there were tears in her eyes; Rolf had not spoken, and she wondered why. What could he be thinking of her? Had she got it all wrong?

When Rolf had recovered some of his composure he said, 'I never realised that falling in love could be so wonderful. The moment I first saw you I had such a strange sensation. Somehow, I knew even then that more than anything in the world I wanted you. There has been so much conflict going on in my mind. My heart has been in a turmoil whenever I've thought of you, my darling, and there has been scarcely a moment when I have not been thinking of you.'

Daphne alarmed him by saying, 'The reason I wanted to see you was to tell you that I couldn't go to Germany with you.'

'Oh, but Daphne, why not?' he cried. When she saw the look of utter despair on his face she hastened to reassure him.

'It's all right, dear, I am coming with you.' She could never, as matters had stood earlier, have told him why she did not wish to go, but now she was able to explain.

'It would have been an impossible situation. I was hopelessly in love with you and, not knowing how you felt about me, I should have been useless as a companion to Mrs Bell, and eventually an embarrassment to you. It didn't seem possible that you could love me as I love you, but now that I know that you do love me, I just want to be with you wherever you are.'

They walked back to the house hand-in-hand, their faces radiant with happiness. When Chris saw them he immediately knew that something had happened, but he wisely passed no comment.

'If you two are doing nothing special this evening, why don't you come out with Kitty and me? We can perhaps go for a meal somewhere.'

Daphne looked at Rolf with an expression of agreement. He said, 'Yes, Chris, that's a great idea.'

With a sudden faraway look in her eyes, Daphne with a beguiling smile on her face said, 'Could we go to The Rose Garden?'

'What an inspired suggestion,' Chris said. 'Kitty will be pleased.'

22

There was peace on Ashdown Forest. The last of the picnickers had gone home; a lone fox ambled warily from the trees in the area of King's Standing. In the distance, a fallow deer stood sentinel while the rest of the herd grazed contentedly; the animal kingdom was resuming its sovereignty over the forest; but not entirely. The tranquillity of the evening was rudely shattered by the sound of approaching motor cars. There were two of them; the first of them turned off the main road towards a grassy area surrounded by gorse bushes which had for years provided seclusion for a host of clandestine gatherings. Peter Frobisher was the sole occupant of the car. The second vehicle followed after it; its occupants were Miles Ritchie, Bob Ganton, Ben Wilkie and Fred Lepton.

They left their cars and walked to a small clearing they each knew well. Frobisher perched himself on his shooting stick; the others gathered round him, crouching on the dry grass.

'The reason I've called you all together,' Frobisher said, 'is because we have almost reached the final phase of the Maresfield Park operation. Tomorrow night we dig our last hole, or perhaps I should say we uncover our last hole. The digging has already been done for us; the box we have been seeking has been found. It just remains for us to remove the loose soil, raise it from the hole and then move it quickly.'

'Where is this 'ere 'ole?' Ben Wilkie wanted to know.

''old yer mouth,' rasped Miles Ritchie. 'Wait till the guvnor's finished.'

'We shall meet in the church car park tomorrow evening at ten o'clock sharp,' Frobisher continued. 'Miles, you will find the necessary tools in the boot of young Pattaway's car which will be in the car park when you arrive. I shall supply you with a folding trolley; I shall then, and not until then, direct you to the place where you are to go to find the hole. When you have unearthed the box it will be mounted on the trolley and brought to the car park where I shall be waiting. You will load it into the boot of my car; Wilkie and Lepton will ride with me and you will take Ganton and follow in Pattaway's car. When we have reached our destination the box will be unloaded and taken to a place I shall indicate when we arrive. When the box has been safely delivered, you will each be given five thousand pounds and will go on your way. Are there any questions?'

Miles Ritchie wanted to know, 'What are we doin' about young Pattaway: will 'e be comin' with us?'

'I shall be seeing him earlier in the evening,' Frobisher answered. 'I'll pay him off then, and tell him to make his own way back to Crawley.'

'What abaht my brother; 'ow's 'e gonner be paid?' Ritchie demanded to know.

With a look of scorn, Frobisher turned on him and said, 'Your brother is inside, and so is Richardson. People who are stupid enough to attract police attention are of no earthly use to me. It was agreed by our benefactor that only those who stayed with us to the end would be rewarded; if you want to give him half of what you get, that's your affair. The pair of them asked for what's coming to them; had they been caught doing work for me, that would have been a totally different matter.'

In another part of the forest, plans were being made for the reception of the chest; by tomorrow night it should be safely in the hands of the man who had plotted and schemed for its recovery from the ground where it had so long been hidden. He had drawn from his personal bank account in London, a large sum of money so that Peter Frobisher could pay off his workers. When he had first heard that the young German had arrived in the village, he had been infuriated at the possiblity of interference, but Peter Frobisher had handled the situation admirably, and would be suitably rewarded.

What a stroke of good fortune it had been that one of his companies had been engaged to handle the disposal of furnishings from Maresfield Park mansion. In the drawer of a bureau, one of the workmen had discovered a copy of the inventory of all the objects of value, and this had been presented to him as a matter of interest. It was only a copy, but it had led him to speculate as to the whereabouts of the items on the list. He felt that the potential value at today's market prices would be incalculable.

Had he been too generous in agreeing to let Frobisher have a quarter of the contents? It would certainly make him a very wealthy man. No, he would be fair to the man; after all, it was he who had discovered, through the disclosure of a garrulous gardener he had employed, that a chest had been hidden in The Park. The gardener, Ben Wilkie, had got the story from his wife whose grandfather, Eli Parkin, had been one of the party of workmen who had buried it. Although he had had no idea of what area of The Park it was in, old Eli had recognised the distinctive smell of oaks, and the smell had lingered in his memory.

For a long time, the organiser had been hoping to get away from the commercial scene and find a comfortable tax haven in a warm climate, but the miserable performance of some of his companies had prevented this happening. Now, at last, he was going to be able to do all the things he had dreamed of. Iris was ready for a move. She had been by no means fulfilled during the time they had lived in Sussex.

On Tuesday evening Alan Pattaway arrived at the church car park a quarter of an hour early for his eight o'clock rendezvous; he was surprised to see that his contact was already waiting for him. He wondered if he'd got the time wrong, and half expected a ticking off for his unpunctuality. He looked again at his watch, and then for confirmation he glanced over at the church clock. No, he wasn't late and he didn't get a ticking off.

The greeting was most cordial, and he was delighted when he was handed two bundles of notes, each containing £1,000.

'Half of this,' he was told, 'is in recognition of the information you have been able to supply. The other half is an offer for your car which I hope you will accept. It happens that I have a requirement for such a car, and if you will just hand over the keys, I'm sure you'll be able to make your own way back to Crawley or wherever it is. If you'll take my advice you'll get as far away from here as possible, and forget that we ever met.'

23

Chris and Rolf were at Holmwood, where Raymond Glover was going over with them details of plans the police had devised for what they were calling Operation Park Watch.

'We can't be sure as to when the digging will take place,' said Raymond, 'so the police are already keeping a round-the-clock watch in the neighbourhood. There's been a workman on the church tower for most of today; he has an unrestricted view of the middle drive up to and beyond Colbridge and he's in touch by radio with the Uckfield police station. There's an unmarked car half a mile along the road out to Nutley, another along the Uckfield road and yet another near the Piltdown crossroads. After dark the onus will be on you two chaps to keep the site under observation, and to telephone me as soon as the diggers enter the grounds at Colbridge.'

As he was speaking, the telephone rang. It was answered by Mrs Glover.

'It's the police station for you, darling,' Connie said.

Raymond took the instrument and spoke to the desk sergeant. When he had finished his conversation, he came back and said, 'A car has been left in the church car park for over an hour. It's an old Ford Consul. Two men were seen to leave it. One of them went towards *The Chequers* and the other man walked into *The Park*.'

'That sounds to me like Alan's car,' said Chris. 'One of us should perhaps go along to *The Chequers* and see if he's left a message.'

'I'll go,' said Rolf. He lost no time in making his way down to the village. When he arrived at *The Chequers* he went up to his room to see if any message had been left, but there was none.

Rolf went down to the bar. Charles Broxon was standing alone at the end of the bar counter.

'Hello, Rolf,' Charles said. 'You've just missed the excitement.'

'What was that?' Rolf asked.

'I've just had to ask a customer to leave. He was throwing money around like water, but when I considered he'd had enough to drink, I told Nancy to stop serving him. He was no more than a youth. In fact, he seemed quite a decent youngster, but he wanted to fight. I almost had to carry him to the door. When he first came in, he was my only customer and he was talking quite amiably with Nancy. He had just sold his car, he told her.'

'You've no idea which way he went?' Rolf queried.

'No', Charles replied, 'but he did say earlier on that he had to get back to Crawley.'

Rolf left the inn and looked round the back. He then walked round the churchyard and into the car park. There was no sign of Alan, but the car was still there. He walked back to Holmwood and told Raymond and Chris what he had heard.

'It sounds very much as though Frobisher has acquired the car,' said Chris, 'and we can guess why.'

'Yes,' Raymond said, 'and it looks as though it's going to happen tonight.'

'We'd better start making a move,' Chris suggested.

It was only a short walk from Holmwood to Colbridge. Chris and Rolf went into the house, switching on the downstairs lights and drawing all the curtains. They then went upstairs and took up observation posts; Chris in a room which had a clear view of the main entrance gates, and Rolf was able from his room to see the site of the hole.

Shortly after ten o'clock, when it was quite dark, Chris spotted the outlines of four figures moving stealthily through the gateway and onto the drive. He called through to Rolf and then went to the telephone to alert Raymond to the fact that things had begun to happen. The four men dispersed, going in different directions, and for a time were out of sight. It was a further ten minutes before Rolf saw a short flash from a torch which he took to be a signal to the other three men. One of the men had apparently discovered the wheelbarrow. Rolf watched, his eyes straining, as the men converged on the site. Chris joined Rolf and the two of them, with a certain amount of grim satisfaction, kept their vigil, happy in the knowledge that the men were experiencing great difficulty in unearthing the chest.

It was almost an hour before the digging was completed, and a further ten minutes was taken in hauling the chest out of its grave. It was eventually lifted onto a trolley and wheeled towards the gateway. When the men had reached the middle drive, Chris took up the telephone, dialled Raymond Glover's number, let it ring three times, and then he replaced the receiver.

In the church car park, Peter Frobisher waited impatiently for the return of the working party. It was half past eleven when he heard footsteps and the gentle rumble of the heavily laden trolley coming towards him. He opened the boot of his car, and the chest was quickly put in place and made secure. No words were exchanged. Frobisher got into his car accompanied by Wilkie and Lepton; Ganton joined Ritchie in the Consul. The ignition key was already in place, and Ritchie had no difficulty in starting up the engine.

Frobisher led the way, and the Consul fell in behind. They left the church car park, turning left, and left again at the junction taking the East Grinstead Road. They were too excited to take notice of a Rover standing outside The Chequers. This car took the same road as the other two, leaving a gap between them of about a hundred yards.

When Frobisher arrived at Lampool Corner he left the East Grinstead road and turned right towards Ashdown Forest. Ritchie followed and the Rover also took a right turn. Two miles onto the forest they took one of several private roads over the heathland. By this time, the third car was being driven without lights, the driver having decided it was no longer necessary to follow quite so closely. Along this particular road there was but one possible destination, and to his colleague he said, 'You can call them up now. Tell them it's High Platts.'

Frobisher brought his car to a halt in the courtyard; a blaze of light flooded the area, and a door was opened.

Behind him the Consul drew up and the occupants alighted and joined their comrades. The chest was unloaded and carried into a room which was already stacked almost to the ceiling with packing cases. The men were ordered to wait, and Frobisher went to the main door of the house and was immediately admitted. He emerged some time later with a briefcase which he opened in front of the men. He took out four bundles of notes, giving one to each of them. Having satisfied them he said, 'Mr Brown is very grateful to you for all you've done. Now you can go, and keep a low profile for the time being. I'll be in touch with you, Ritchie, when something else turns up.'

The men took their money and piled into the Ford Consul. As they drove back along the private road, they took no notice of the car following behind at a discreet distance; they assumed it was Frobisher. Before they reached the main road they were confronted by a stationary police patrol car, and the Rover drew up behind them to block their retreat. Four burly police officers came up to their car and asked them to get out.

Three of the men alighted from the car and were immediately handcuffed and searched for possible weapons. The fourth, Ritchie, wriggled away from the bunch and dashed off across the heath hotly pursued by the two plain clothes men from the Rover. A second patrol vehicle came on the scene, and the three captives were bundled inside and taken off to the police station. Twenty minutes later the two detectives returned from their chase, which had proved fruitless. Ritchie had managed to evade capture. One of the constables took the Consul into Uckfield to be impounded. The two plain clothes men drove back towards High Platts, getting as near to the house as possible in order to observe any activity there might be.

Sir Harold Grantwell and Peter Frobisher crossed the courtyard, armed with a heavy hammer and a crowbar. The detectives called up the men in the patrol car, who coasted quietly down towards the big house. Inside the storeroom, Frobisher was busily attacking the rusty padlocks on the chest. He struggled for ten minutes before the impatient Grantwell took over from him. After a further quarter of an hour, Sir Harold managed to sever the locks from their mountings, and the chest was prised open.

There was a gasp of dismay from Frobisher, and a scream of rage from Grantwell. The noise of cursing and swearing which followed alerted the police officers who immediately moved in, taking the two men completely by surprise. Grantwell swung out wildly with the crowbar, narrowly missing the head of Detective Sergeant Hastings and in doing so, he lost his balance and fell backwards onto the floor. One of the uniformed constables sat on him, taking the wind out of his sails. Frobisher was quickly relieved of the hammer he was wielding, and realised that further resistance would be unwise.

'We'd like to see what you are storing in these cases, sir,' Sergeant Hastings said to Sir Harold.

'On what authority?' demanded Grantwell. 'You know you have no business on these premises without written authority.'

'My my, Sir Harold,' said a fresh voice from the doorway, 'we are in exalted company. We have reason to believe that you may be in possession of articles which are not your own property, and I have a search-warrant signed by a local magistrate, which authorises me to search any part of your premises.' Both Grantwell and Frobisher recognised the speaker as he pulled the search-warrant from his pocket. He was Detective Chief Inspector Tideswell, a fellow member of their golf club.

'Now, sir,' the chief inspector addressed Frobisher, 'are you going to open these cases or do we have to break them open?'

'They're not locked,' Frobisher growled. Two of the constables were instructed to take a few of the packing cases and open them up. They revealed a veritable Aladin's Cave of precious objects, one or two of which the detectives recognised as fitting the description they had of articles recently stolen from houses in the surrounding countryside. They found shipping documents made out in the name of P R FROBISHER and addressed to various parts of the world.

'Right gentlemen,' said the chief inspector, 'I must ask you to accompany me to the station.'

They were duly cautioned and taken to the police station at Uckfield where they were charged with being in possession of stolen goods, and given basic accommodation for the night.

24

Early on Wednesday morning, Chris and Rolf made their way to Holmwood, where Kitty had prepared a huge breakfast for them. Raymond joined them and together they speculated on the outcome of Operation Park Watch. They did not have to speculate for long. Before they had finished their breakfast, the telephone rang and Kitty answered it and called her father over.

'Raymond Glover speaking. Yes, hello Derek; haven't you been to bed? Oh yes; they're both with me now. Good heavens; I can't believe it.'

Chris and Rolf were itching to know what it was that Raymond couldn't believe, but they had to wait at least ten minutes before he returned to the table.

'That was Detective Chief Inspector Derek Tideswell of the county police. He's over the moon with the night's work. He says he wants to meet the two men who were instrumental in setting it up.'

'Yes,' said Chris impatiently, 'but we'd really like to know what happened.'

'They've taken Frobisher into custody, and you'll never guess who is his partner in crime.'

The two men were irritated, knowing the futility of trying to guess. 'It's Sir Harold Grantwell,' he told them. 'Frobisher and his men were tailed to High Platts. Three of the men were picked up on the forest, but the fourth one, Ritchie, got away. One of Grantwell's outhouses has been used as a warehouse for almost every burglary there's been over the past year or so.

'They are all being held at the police station, and Grantwell and Frobisher have been charged with receiving, but that's only one of the charges they'll be facing. They've both been in contact with their solicitors

159

who will be travelling down from London during the morning. There'll be a special hearing later on, after the legal men have had time to talk things over with their clients. The police will oppose any application for bail.'

The three men finished breakfast, and while Chris gave Kitty a hand with the dishes, Raymond took Rolf to one side and said, 'I don't know how to put this, Rolf, but one of the things Derek Tideswell told me, affects you. It appears that the chest these people have been digging for, and of course the one in which you had an interest, was unearthed over fifty years ago. It was hushed up at the time in order to avoid a major diplomatic incident, and consequently nothing appeared in the newspapers.' Rolf spent a few moments in silent contemplation, not knowing what to say. Then he held his sides and began to rock with laughter.

Chris and Kitty stopped what they were doing and rushed into the room. They had to wait four or five minutes for Rolf to regain his composure sufficiently to speak to them.

'What is it, Rolf? What's come over you?' Chris asked anxiously.

'The treasure, Chris, the buried treasure!' Rolf mouthed rather than spoke the words.

'Yes, Rolf, what about it?' Chris persisted.

'There isn't any!' and having said this, Rolf again collapsed into a paroxysm of uncontrollable mirth.

Raymond, in order to spare Chris further anxiety, explained the situation, repeating what he had just told Rolf. Chris digested the information and waited until Rolf was ready to join in the conversation.

'You don't appear to be terribly disappointed,' Chris said at last.

'I just can't tell you how relieved I am,' Rolf replied.

There was a hole to be filled in, and Chris and Rolf returned to Colbridge and set about the task with a will. Rolf felt that he had done all that could be expected of him in fulfilling the promise he had made to his grandfather, and somehow, the filling in of this hole seemed to symbolise the sealing of the covenant.

Chris suggested, after the task was completed, that Rolf

should accompany him to have coffee with his parents in order to put them in the picture. He felt that it was hardly fair for them to have to hear it through the press or on local radio, and so they lost no time in making their way to the Charnfords.

Kitty's smart little red Spitfire sports car was parked in the drive, and Daphne was just on the point of getting in alongside her friend.

When the girls saw the two men arriving, they decided spontaneously that they were not going anywhere. They left the car, making their way over to where the Jaguar was coming to a halt. Kitty took Chris by the arm and looked up at him adoringly, waiting to be kissed. Daphne steered Rolf towards the house, where her parents awaited news of the night's events. Mrs Charnford hastily prepared coffee and when Chris and Kitty came inside, Arthur Charnford also came and joined the party.

Chris waited for Rolf to tell the story, but Rolf thought it better that his friend should put his family in the picture.

'You'll never guess who's been sponsoring Frobisher, Dad; Sir Harold Grantwell.'

'No, Chris, surely not Grantwell,' said his father.

'Yes, and what's more, there's a whole hoard of valuable antiques up at High Platts which will take some explaining. The police have managed to identify several items on their list of articles missing as a result of recent burglaries in the Kent and East Sussex area, and that after examining only two or three cases. There's another twenty or so to be gone through yet. They are all neatly packed and labelled ready for shipment overseas. Apart from Grantwell and Frobisher, three other men are in custody, but a fourth one managed to get away.'

Rolf put in, 'The man who got away is Miles Ritchie. He's the brother of one of the men who attacked Nancy from *The Chequers*. From what is known of him, he's probably the most dangerous.'

'Isn't he the man who's supposed to be gunning for you, Rolf?' Arthur asked.

'Oh yes, that's the fellow,' Rolf replied, 'but I imagine

he'll be too concerned with protecting his own hide to bother about me.' Arthur and his wife raised eyebrows simultaneously as their daughter gave a little murmur of apprehension.

'Do take special care, Rolf,' Daphne said. 'I don't want anything to happen to you.'

Her parents shared with all of them concern for Rolf's safety, as was only natural, but somehow Daphne's outburst seemed to indicate a much more personal concern. Was she growing even more fond of the young man than they had suspected, and if so, was the feeling reciprocated? It was all rather too soon in their acquaintance with the young fellow for them to conceive of any romantic attachment. They had no objection, of course; Rolf was a delightful young man, and they would be proud to welcome him into the family if in due course they saw any sign of Rolf himself being more than a little romantically attracted towards her.

They pushed it to the back of their minds, and waited to hear more of what the two young men had to say.

'The holes they have been digging have all been a complete waste of time,' said Chris. 'There is no buried treasure. Kitty's father has been advised by the police that it was found over fifty years ago but for diplomatic reasons, nothing was ever published in the newspapers or on radio.'

'You don't seem particularly worried, Rolf,' Arthur Charnford observed.

'No, I'm not, Mr Charnford,' Rolf declared, 'Just think of all the problems I should have had if I'd found it. Now I have no problems; I can enjoy the rest of my time in England. That is not to say I have not enjoyed the time I have been here already; it has been wonderful. I have enjoyed the beautiful countryside, marvellous hospitality and I have made many friendships, and I have lost my heart to the most beautiful and adorable girl in the world.'

A long silence followed Rolf's declaration. The Charnfords were stunned. The young man was the first to speak; his voice was unsteady and his face showed visible signs of distress. He rose to his feet and said, 'I am so very sorry if I have offended you; I apologise for my incorrect behaviour, but my heart is overflowing with happiness and I just had to give voice to my feelings. Please forgive me.'

Daphne went and stood beside him and looked up into his face. Tears of joy were in her eyes as she said, 'It's all right, darling!' Sylvia Charnford spoke up, 'We are very happy for you both and you have our blessing. Don't they, Arthur?'

'Oh, yes, of course,' Arthur replied. 'this isn't the way I've always imagined it would be. You've certainly taken us by surprise.'

'Perhaps,' said Rolf, ' I ought to leave you now and give you chance to get used to the idea. If you will excuse me, I'll be getting back to The Chequers.'

Daphne accompanied him a short way down the drive, hanging on to his arm and saying, 'Oh Rolf, I had no idea your feelings were so strong. Are you quite sure you meant what you said?'

'Yes, Daphne, I have never been so sure of anything, but you don't have to commit yourself. I can be patient and give you time to consider the situation.'

'I don't need time, Rolf,' she whispered, 'I've felt the same about you since the first day we met, but I didn't dare to let you know in case you weren't interested in me.'

They walked on a little further until they were out of sight of the house and Rolf took her in his arms and showed her just how interested he was.

'Rolf has taken me almost as much by surprise as he has you,'
Daphne said when she returned to see her parents looking staggered and bemused. 'I had no idea he felt that way about me.'

'And what about you, my love. How do you feel?' her father asked.

'I love him dearly, Daddy, but I couldn't show it before. It has taken a lot of effort on my part, I can tell you, but I couldn't let the family down, could I? But don't start hearing wedding bells yet. I shall be meeting his parents next week when we take Mrs Bell over there, but this puts a different complexion on things. They may not like me, nor I them, and that would cause a setback.'

'You'll need time really to get to know one another,' said her mother. 'There's so much more to marriage than making love and remember, whatever the modern generation's attitude to marriage may be, the backbone of civilised society is family, and it's up to the young people to realise their responsibility to future generations, and to establish their lives together on a firm foundation. Now, having said all that, I know that your judgment is sound. We like Rolf, and now that we know how you both feel, we'll prepare ourselves for the happy day, when it comes. Enjoy your courtship. It's a most wonderful time of your lives together and, conducted honourably and morally, prepares you for even more wonderful experiences in your future married life.'

'Thank you, Mummy,' said Daphne, 'I know what you're saying, and I just hope that our marriage, when it happens, will be like yours and Daddy's.'

Although Chris and Kitty remained in the background, they had not been unaware of the dialogue that had occupied the rest of the family and they were in their own way, thrilled at what they had heard. Kitty couldn't wait to get Daphne on her own, and Chris felt he wanted to go and congratulate Rolf, but he knew it would be better to let matters take their course without any interference from him. Rolf was a tremendous chap to have as a friend, and he could think of no one he'd rather have as a brother-in-law, but it was early days yet.

Daphne wandered off into the garden and had not returned when Kitty was ready to go home, so it looked as though there would be no exchanges of confidences just yet.

25

When Rolf returned to *The Chequers* the bar was crowded. To many of the villagers, the inn was the focal point of their social life, and it seemed natural for them to gather there whenever something momentous was happening. No one appeared to be in full possession of the facts, and so rumour and speculation were rife. What was known was that there had been a great amount of police activity throughout the night and it had been centred on Ashdown Forest. Several people had been arrested, and apparently they included a person of some importance.

No one appeared to know who this person was, but several wild guesses were being made, and some of the more garrulous customers were causing Charles Broxon a great deal of embarrassment. No one who was anyone was being spared, and it seemed that the only way to be eliminated from the list of possibilities was to appear in person at *The Chequers* in full view of the speculators.

Meanwhile the consumption of alcohol was gratifying to the landlord, and Charles and Nancy's efforts were reinforced by the assistance of Alice, the Broxons' daily help. It was most unusual for Alice to be seen behind the bar, and she was not at all sure that her Albert would approve. However, she was spurred on by the prospect of a generous manifestation of Charles Broxon's gratitude at the end of the week. The extra money would come in useful when she would have to buy shoes for the children starting back to school.

Pat Broxon was kept busy preparing bar snacks, as many of the customers were reluctant to leave the premises a moment before time. Rolf availed himself of a ploughman's lunch which was served in his room. After he had finished eating he made his way down to the reception desk and put a call through to London. Mrs Colbey's niece answered the call, and apologised for the fact that her aunt and uncle, along with her mother, were out of the house and were not expected back until the early part of the evening.

'May I ask who is calling please?' she enquired.

'Yes, of course,' the young man answered, 'my name is Muller; Rolf Muller.'

'Oh, Mr Muller,' she said, 'Uncle Roger told me there might possibly be a call from either yourself or Chris Charnford. He'll be sorry he's missed you. Is there a number he can call you back on?'

'If he can ring after nine o'clock we'll both be at his house,' Rolf said, and with a light-hearted chuckle he added, 'I'm sure he knows the number.'

'How is Chris keeping these days?' asked Helen.

'He's keeping very well indeed,' Rolf replied.

'Have you met Daphne?' he was asked.

'Yes I have, and she too is extremely well,' he told her. 'Do give her my love,' Helen requested, 'and tell her I'm sorry I haven't been in touch. I'm sure she'll understand if you tell her there's someone very special who takes up all my spare time.'

Feeling that it was only fair to let Martin Bell know all the latest news, Rolf took a walk down to his cottage, knocked on the door and was invited by Mrs Bell to go inside.

'Good afternoon, Mr Muller,' Grace said, 'it's good to see you. I'm sorry Martin's out at the moment, but it shouldn't be long before he's back. He's gone to Turley's to get a few groceries. Do take a seat. Now, how about a nice cup of tea, or would you rather wait until Martin gets back?'

Rolf was on the point of replying when the door opened and Martin came in.

'Hello, Mr Muller,' he said, 'nice of you to call. I'll just put the kettle on. Sorry I've been away so long, Grace, but you know how difficult it is to get away from George Turley.'

Martin made a pot of tea and poured out three cups

before sitting down with his wife and their visitor.

'Let me bring you up-to-date with what has happened,' Rolf said. 'First of all, let me tell you there is no treasure. Apparently it was discovered fifty years ago, but it has been kept very quiet.'

'Really,' Martin said in amazement, 'strange we never heard about it.'

Rolf did not enlarge on what he had already said concerning the chest but he went on, 'The police had a very successful night's work. Altogether five people have been arrested, and they include our friend, Peter Frobisher, and Sir Harold Grantwell.'

'Surely not Sir Harold!' Mrs Bell gasped.

Rolf continued, 'A whole lot of valuables have been discovered at the home of Sir Harold, and the police have been able to identify several items as having been stolen. We'd better not talk about it too much yet, but no doubt the papers will be full of it by tomorrow.'

Martin joined in and told Grace and Rolf about the gossip currently circulating in the village, and centred on Turley's. It was very similar to what Rolf had already heard, with just one difference; a customer at the shop had been so indiscreet as to name the important personage as Commander Brewster. It appeared that neither Turley's store nor The Chequers had been able to come up with evidence as to the precise nature of the offences committed.

Chris was already at Colbridge by the time Rolf arrived. 'Kitty and Daphne are calling round later on,' Chris said. 'They are at a meeting in the rectory to discuss the final arrangements for the fte on Saturday.'

Rolf's face lit up, and the change was not lost on Chris who added, 'I though you'd be pleased. By the way, Rolf, Mr Colbey rang just a few minutes ago. He was unable to wait until nine o'clock as he was going out with some friends. I was able to give him the news, but do you know, he wasn't a bit surprised when I told him that the chest had been unearthed several years ago? He was surprised however when I told him about Frobisher and Grantwell.'

'I've been down to see Martin Bell,' Rolf said. 'He had heard rumours which have been circulating at Turley's and *The Chequers* at lunchtime. Have you heard anything more, Chris?'

'Frobisher and Grantwell appeared in court this afternoon,' Chris said. 'They had their application for bail turned down, and they've both been remanded in custody for three weeks to enable the police to make further investigations. In the meantime, the police are very busy hunting for Miles Ritchie. Does it make you feel uneasy at all? I mean, with the threats he's been making, he may be redoubling his efforts to get at you.'

'I should have thought,' said Rolf, 'that Mr Ritchie would want to get as far away from Maresfield as ever possible.'

A ring on the doorbell was answered by Chris, who returned accompanied by Kitty and Daphne.

By the time they had eaten the meal which the girls prepared, it was getting quite late and, leaving Rolf to look after the house, Chris escorted Kitty the short distance to Holmwood and then drove his sister home. None of them noticed as they were leaving, the figure of a man lurking in the shrubbery. It had not occurred to any of them to draw the curtains, and their every move had been observed. It was apparent to the prowler that Rolf was now alone in the house. Ritchie's reason for being in the grounds of Colbridge had nothing to do with his self-imposed vendetta against the young German.

During the operations the previous evening, he had noticed with particular interest that there was an outhouse near the scene of the digging operations, and when he had made his escape from the police, he made his way back to Colbridge and broke into the hut. He now had an urgent need of food, and it was his intention to break into the house without disturbing the elderly residents. What he had not bargained for was an encounter with four healthy, physically fit young people.

It was with a sense of relief that Ritchie watched Chris and the two girls leaving the house. That meant only the German to be dealt with and he could scarcely believe his good fortune. He was in no hurry to go into action; this golden opportunity for revenge had to be exploited to the full. He saw no point in having a direct confrontation with the man who had already proved his usefulness with his fists. He appreciated that sooner or later, the police would catch up with him, but before that happened, his brother was going to be avenged.

Ritchie made an inspection of the outside of the house, looking for possible faulty window fastenings, but he was not able to find any, nor did he seriously expect to do so. He made his way over to the garden shed where he selected a hefty piece of wood to use as a club. Approaching the front door of the house, he rang the door bell and stepped behind one of the concrete pillars of the portico.

As Rolf went to answer the door, he switched on the outside lights. He opened the door and, seeing no one there he called, 'Who's there?' Getting no response, he took a step forward in order to see who had rung the bell. As he did so, he saw out of the corner of his eye the shadow of a man with his hand raised, holding a cudgel. Rolf froze in his tracks, leaving the intruder to make the next move. When after five minutes no move was made, Rolf edged towards the pillar, not for a moment taking his eye off the shadow. Suddenly the cudgel was drawn backwards and swung in an arc towards the back of Rolf's head. As the blow was about to make contact, Rolf stepped nimbly to one side and at the same time he made a grab for the arm of the villain. Taken completely by surprise, the man lost his balance, giving the young German the opportunity to hurl him to the ground.

The headlights of the Jaguar sweeping up the drive revealed the astonishing sight of the two men rolling about on the ground, one clutching firmly on to the wooden club, and the other struggling to wrest it from his grasp. Chris brought the car to a halt and got out in time to see the man with the club jumping to his feet and starting to make a run for it. Sizing up the situation in an instant, he made a flying tackle and brought the man down flat on his face.

A telephone call to the police station brought a squad car round to the house within minutes. A very subdued Miles Ritchie was bundled into the vehicle and taken down to Uckfield to be formally charged.

Left to themselves, Chris and Rolf retired to the comfort of the drawing-room to take stock of the injuries incurred. Rolf's jacket was badly torn. He removed it and rolled back his sleeve to reveal on his left arm the beginning of a bruise just above the wrist, and a badly grazed elbow. Chris had ruined his trousers in making the tackle on Ritchie, but was otherwise none the worse for his brave participation in the fracas. A temporary dressing was applied to Rolf's wounds, and a large brandy each served to put them in the right frame of mind for a well-earned night's rest.

26

On Thursday morning Chris and Rolf were invited to visit the police station at Uckfield, where brief statements were taken from them. Sergeant Graham was in a jovial mood, referring to them as the Maresfield Vigilantes. To Chris, however, there appeared to be a note of irony in his voice. The police had spent months trying to track down the gang responsible for the burglaries which had plagued the area, all without success. These two amateurs had come along and had instigated the operation which had led to the capture of the entire gang.

The two friends decided to lunch together, and spent a relaxing two hours at *The Maiden's Head* in Uckfield, rather than risking the inevitable questioning they would have had to endure had they returned to *The Chequers*.

As they were driving back to Maresfield, Roger and Beryl Colbey were both slightly apprehensive as to what they might find at Colbridge. It was not that they harboured any doubts as to the way the two young stalwarts might have acquitted themselves during their period of stewardship. They were unaware of the additional activity in which the young men had been involved the previous evening. It was just that their neighbour, Peter Frobisher, had turned out to be a criminal; it was beyond their comprehension. Of Sir Harold Grantwell, they knew very little, although Lady Grantwell had acquired for herself a certain reputation in the surrounding countryside as a prolific charity organiser.

Would things ever be the same again? Colbey wondered; whoever would have thought of anyone living in The Park being capable of conduct so reprehensible as to take a neighbour's property? What will Chris

Charnford and the young German think of me when they learn that I knew all along that there was no treasure to be found? On the other hand, I suppose if I hadn't allowed the digging to go ahead, they would never have flushed out the den of thieves.

He was still musing in this fashion when he arrived in Maresfield. As he neared The Limes, he saw Rolf Muller who was on his way to visit the Briggs', and was just about to walk through the gateway of The Limes. As Roger drew level with the young man he brought the car to a halt and hailed him. 'Hello, Mr Muller.'

'Good afternoon, sir,' Rolf replied. 'I trust you had an enjoyable stay in London.'

'Thank you, yes; it was most enjoyable. But what about you? Will you have time to call on us this evening?' Roger enquired.

'I'm calling on Colonel and Mrs Briggs now. Perhaps I could call on you later this afternoon after I leave them.'

The Colbeys continued on their way home and Rolf walked towards the Briggs' front door. Mrs Briggs expressed her delight at seeing the young man again, and led him into the drawing-room where the colonel was sitting browsing through The Times.

'My dear chap, how good of you to spare the time to come and brighten up our day. You've no idea what this means to us.'

'I hope you will forgive me if I stay for only a short time,' Rolf said, 'but I have so many things to do, and I have promised to visit the Colbeys later this afternoon.'

Mrs Briggs brought in a tray with tea and cakes, she sat down with the two men and poured tea from a fine Georgian silver teapot into cups of the most exquisite Minton china. Just as she had finished pouring tea there was a ring on the front door bell. In the absence of Mrs Jones, Maude herself went to answer it. Rolf immediately recognised the voice of Daphne Charnford. What was being said, he had no idea. The conversation went on for some time, but there was an unmistakable note of protest when eventually Mrs Briggs returned to the drawing-room accompanied by a reluctant Daphne. The reluctance quickly gave way to a look of pleasure as she saw Rolf rising from his seat, together with a somewhat more formal Colonel Briggs.

'Come in, my dear; how perfectly delightful to see you. You know Mr Muller, don't you?' the colonel queried. It was obvious from their greeting that the question was superfluous.

'Good afternoon, Colonel Briggs,' Daphne replied. 'I'm so sorry to intrude; I simply came round on a small errand for Mummy. Hello Rolf.'

Thinking of nothing more suitable to say he said, 'Hello.'

Ignoring the possibility of further protest, Mrs Briggs produced an extra cup and saucer for Daphne and insisted that she join them. Daphne took what she now considered to be her rightful place at Rolf's side and showed no sign of embarrassment as she took his hand and held it rather longer than convention demanded.

'It appears that there's been some sort of excitement going on in the village,' Colonel Briggs said. 'I don't know what it is exactly. Have you heard anything, Daphne?'

Daphne looked at Rolf, and asked him, 'Can we tell them?'

'I don't see why not,' Rolf replied. 'It will be in the evening newspapers and on the radio I've no doubt.'

'Prepare yourselves for a shock, Colonel,' Daphne said. 'Mr Frobisher and Sir Harold Grantwell have been arrested by the police, along with four other men who were working with them.'

'Good heavens!' spluttered the colonel. 'What on earth have they been up to?'

'It is not for us to say, sir,' Rolf answered, 'but I understand that the police have discovered a whole lot of valuable antiques at the home of Sir Harold, and many of them will be readily identified by residents in the county.'

'Are you telling me that my neighbour is a villain?' The colonel did not wait for an answer. 'No, of course you're not. Wouldn't do at all, would it. But by Jove, come to think of it . . .' Maude interrupted, 'No dear, the less we say, the better. No doubt all will be revealed in time, and in the meantime, we have guests in the house.'

'This fruitcake is delicious,' Daphne said in a valiant

attempt to relieve the tension.

'Thank you, Daphne; I baked it myself along with a few others for the cake stall on Saturday,' said Mrs Briggs. 'Oh! talking of the cake stall, Doris Frobisher is in charge of it. I wonder if she'll be there, in view of Peter's predicament.'

'I should hardly think so,' murmured Daphne. 'Fortunately there are plenty of other ladies who are wanting to help. No doubt the rector will be able to arrange a substitute.'

As Rolf and Daphne left The Limes together, she reminded him that he was to pick her up at seven o'clock. Her car was parked on the drive, and as she got in she threw him a kiss and he made his way on foot to Colbridge which was but a short walk away. He was met at the door by Roger who took him inside to where Beryl was sitting in front of a coffee table.

'You'll have a cup of tea, Mr Muller, won't you?' she asked him. He felt it would be churlish to refuse, even though he had just had tea at The Limes.

Beryl went to the kitchen to put the kettle on. While the two men were alone Roger Colbey said, 'You've done a tremendous service to this community, Mr Muller.'

Before Rolf could respond he carried on, 'and I have to apologise to you for my shameful behaviour in allowing you to search for a chest which I knew was no longer to be found. Will you ever be able to forgive me?'

'Think no more about it, sir; I heard about it yesterday, and have had enough time to come to terms with the situation,' said Rolf.

'I must say, it gave me quite a shock to hear that my neighbour Frobisher was involved. As for Grantwell, I don't know much about him; I've only met him a couple of times. He didn't strike me as being the sort of fellow I'd want as a friend, nor yet as an enemy.'

'I met him once, riding on the forest,' Rolf said; 'Chris Charnford introduced us. I took an instant dislike to him.'

Mrs Colbey came in with tea but Rolf reluctantly declined to eat anything. 'I've been given instructions that I must do nothing to take the edge off my appetite, but I have no idea why.' The two Colbeys exchanged glances, and did not pursue the matter further.   'We should very much have liked you to come and have a meal with us,' Mrs Colbey said, 'but I should imagine the short time you have left here in Maresfield will be pretty well taken up.'

'I fear that is so, Mrs Colbey; I shall be returning to Germany on Monday of next week, but I hope to return again quite soon.'

Rolf would have liked to have prolonged his visit, but he had several things to do before going to the Charnfords. As he walked towards the village, he encountered the rector who asked him if he could spare a few moments of his time. Rolf walked back with him as far as the rectory, but would not go inside, explaining that he was pressed for time.

'I wonder if you could give us some assistance tomorrow,' the rector wanted to know. 'We're terribly short of willing hands to help with the erection of tents and marquees. I've just been round to ask Peter Frobisher if he could help, but I couldn't make anyone hear. I suppose you'll think I have an awful cheek to ask you, but I'm becoming quite desperate.'

'Not at all, sir, I shall be very happy to help you,' said Rolf. 'Have you thought of asking Chris Charnford?'

'Why no, I haven't,' said the rector, 'I wonder if he would help.'

'I shall be seeing him shortly,' Rolf said, 'I'll put it to him.'

'I'm most grateful to you, Mr Muller; we shall be starting about ten o'clock,' the rector said.

Rolf was pleased to be able to help the rector, but was relieved that this particular little chat had not lasted too long. He continued on his way and, arriving at The Chequers, he was met at the door by Charles Broxon. With him was a young man in uniform.   'Rolf,' said Charles, 'I'd like you to meet my son, Ted.'

Rolf put out his hand and said, 'I'm very pleased to meet you, Ted.'

'I'm delighted to meet you, sir,' said the young soldier. 'I've been told so much about you, and I want to thank you for what you did for Nancy.'

'I was pleased to have been in the right place at the

right time,'   Rolf said. 'Beyond that, it was a privilege.'

In an effort to turn the conversation away from himself Rolf asked, 'How do you like being in Germany?'

'I find it very little different from being in England in many ways. At first it was interesting to travel around. I've seen some of the lovely old towns, and I've had one or two short leaves in the Harz Mountains, but after a time it becomes just like any other military posting. All I look forward to now is being at home with the family and, of course, with Nancy. I've been posted back to England, so I shall be seeing a lot more of them. Nancy and I are getting married in six weeks time and we should like you to come to the wedding, if you can possibly manage to get here.'

Rolf assured him that he'd make every effort to be there.

Glancing at his watch, Rolf realised that he was short of time and asked Ted to excuse him as he was due out again in just an hour.

27

Rolf raced up to his room, shaved and had a hasty bath. By the time he was ready to go out again, forty minutes had elapsed. Arriving at the Charnfords, he was surprised at the number of cars that were drawn up outside the house. His arrangements with Daphne had been, he thought, purely tentative, although she had for some inexplicable reason insisted that he be there promptly at seven o'clock.

Chris came to the door to let him in, and when the door was opened, Rolf heard the hum of several voices.

'Do I interrupt something?' he asked.

'No,' Chris replied mysteriously, 'come along inside. I'll let Daphne know you're here, but first come along and say hello to everybody.'

Reluctantly, Rolf allowed himself to be ushered into the large drawing-room where Arthur and Sylvia Charnford were entertaining a horde of people. They turned aside from their guests and gave him a hearty greeting.

'I think you know everybody here, Rolf' said Mr Charnford.

The faces turned towards him were all familiar. The Briggs', the Colbeys, the Glovers, the Truscotts, Verity and Prudence Smythe and Martin Bell. As Rolf was getting over his confusion, Charles and Pat Broxon came through the door to complete the gathering.

A schooner of amontillado was put into Rolf's hand. He saw Kitty going over to Chris in a far corner of the room. She put her arm into his, looking adoringly up into his face. Suddenly Rolf became aware of a hand sliding into his own and, looking round, he saw Daphne standing at his side.

'Don't scold me, Rolf,' she laughed. 'I wanted to warn

177

you, but Dad threatened me not to tell you what was happening, and everyone else was sworn to secrecy. I hope you're not too embarrassed.'

How could he possibly scold her? She looked absolutely radiant in a gown of royal blue satin which enhanced the soft whiteness of her skin and the soft shining gold of her hair. She wore no jewellery other than a small golden locket at her neck. It thrilled Rolf to see her. He felt a choke in his throat, and tears came into his eyes; he was totally captivated. The smile she turned on him was one of pure, unadulterated love.

There was a call for silence. Arthur Charnford cleared his throat and began, 'My dear friends, you all know why we are here. All, that is, with one exception, and I hasten now to remedy that necessary omission.' He turned to the young German and said, 'Rolf, from what we know of you, had you been aware of what has been arranged, you would not have been here tonight. We who are here are representative of many people in the village of Maresfield and the surrounding countryside who have reason to thank God for sending you here. For a long time, people have been unable to sleep easily, owing to the number of burglaries which have plagued the countryside of East Sussex. Now, thanks largely to your efforts, the people responsible for these burglaries have been brought to justice.'

'To show our gratitude, we have prepared a dinner in your honour. It has all been done at very short notice, and none of the guests here have had more than three or four hours to respond to the invitation. Later on, we shall ask everyone to drink a toast to you, but first, ladies and gentlemen, will you please take your seats in the dining-room.'

Rolf was intrigued and faintly amused when he thought of the amount of secrecy that had been observed. How such an event could have been organised in so little time was beyond his comprehension; obviously, a lot of hard work had been involved. Mrs Charnford had requested that none of their guests wore formal dinner dress as Rolf would be unprepared for the occasion, and therefore at a disadvantage. Even so, the ladies in particular were very elegant; apart from Daphne, Kitty in shimmering white, looked a perfect English rose.

The guests took their places at the table. An egg mayonnaise already set out in front of them was accompanied by a pleasant English white wine obtained from a local Sussex vineyard. The main course consisted of Coq au vin with sauté and cream potatoes, green peas, carrots and courgettes with a choice of Claret or Mosel wine. A fresh fruit salad was followed by a selection of English cheeses.

The meal ended, Colonel Briggs rose from his seat and requested everyone's attention.

'Ladies and Gentlemen, I have been asked to propose a toast. I think I am right in saying that two weeks ago, our young German friend was unknown to any of us. My understanding is that he came to England because of a promise he had made to his late grandfather, a kinsman of Prince Munster, to visit the estate which had held so many happy childhood memories. Alas, the estate as his grandfather had known it, no longer exists. Many a man, confronted by a similar set of circumstances, would have gone home disappointed, disillusioned, and to some extent embittered. Rolf Muller could have been all these things, but he chose to stay for a while, and during that time each one of us has had an opportunity of meeting him, and I think I can safely say that as a result, our lives have been enriched. It is my pleasure to ask you to rise and drink the health of Rolf Muller.'

The guests rose to their feet and joined in, 'Rolf Muller.' When they sat down, Rolf got up to make his response.

'Colonel Briggs, ladies and gentlemen. Reference has been made to the part I played in the apprehension of those responsible for the crimes committed in the neighbourhood. Quite apart from the vital role of the local police force, I have worked in partnership with Chris and Martin, and each one of you has in one way or another, supplied us with information without which, none of this would have been achieved.

'I should also like to pay a warm tribute to a young man who has been of the utmost help to us. His name is Alan

Pattaway. We first met Alan as an adversary; he was on the fringe of the gang. However, we discovered that he was the victim of circumstances, and when we heard his story we were able to win him over to our side. The assistance he gave us was invaluable, and we owe much to him for the risks he was willing to take in feeding us with details of the movements of his associates.

'You have truly honoured me with this excellent dinner, and I am overwhelmed by your kindness. I came to Maresfield as a stranger, and in so short a time I have made the sort of friendships which often take a lifetime to cultivate. Next week I shall be leaving for Germany, but I shall be returning to England at every possible opportunity.' As he said this, he glanced at Daphne and she responded with a sweet smile, a gesture which was not lost on the other guests. There was much more he could have said, but the occasion was not one which called for lengthy speeches, and he sat down to an enthusiastic round of applause.

Coffee was served in the drawing-room and afterwards, as Chris had earlier predicted to Rolf, Mr Charnford produced a selection of brandies, with malmsey for the ladies.

Kitty and Daphne lent a hand in the kitchen while the male guests cornered Rolf and Chris, plying them with questions. Colonel Briggs was intrigued by what Rolf had said concerning Alan Pattaway, and wanted to hear more. Chris elaborated on the circumstances in which Alan had come onto the scene, explaining how they had played cat and mouse with him and trapped him up on the forest. 'He was on the run from the army, but after being sheltered by undesirable characters in London, he had been blackmailed into joining in their activities.' Chris continued, 'We managed to persuade him of the error of his ways, and when we promised to speak up for him to the authorities, there was not a thing he would not do to help us. At the moment we have no idea where he is, but we owe it to him to do something positive.'

'If you do catch up with him,' said Colonel Briggs, 'advise him to give himself up at the first opportunity, and I'll be happy to use my not inconsiderable influence on his behalf.'

Mrs Charnford was attending to the ladies' requirements. Beryl Colbey was telling them of the exciting two days she and her husband had enjoyed in London, thanks to the kindness of Rolf and Chris in offering to keep an eye on things at Colbridge. When Daphne and Kitty returned to the drawing-room they joined the ladies, and the conversation turned to the church fête. Mrs Truscott expressed the hope that the events of the past few days would not adversely affect the attendance.

'On the contrary, Mrs Truscott,' said Maude Briggs, 'your husband's inspired invitation to Mr Muller to open the fête will prove to be an even bigger incentive for people to come than we could ever have imagined.'

It had been a most enjoyable evening and the guests having gone their separate ways, the young ladies persuaded Rolf and Chris to lend a hand in restoring the home to normality. Sylvia Charnford was expressly forbidden to do any more work, and her husband wisely suggested that they retired for the night. As soon as the place had been made tidy, Kitty showing signs of tiredness, asked Chris to take her home. Before they left, Chris made arrangements with Rolf to meet at The Limes next morning to assist with the manual work connected with the fête.

'And now, darling,' murmured Daphne, 'I've got you to myself at last.'

She went over to the large settee and beckoned Rolf to come and sit by her side. He needed no second bidding. Daphne had somehow made time to go to her room and freshen up, adding a dash or two of perfume. Soon they were locked in each other's arms, and she prepared her lips to be kissed. She was not disappointed; he was a warm-blooded man and could not resist such sweet pleasure. It was a thrill to hold this beautiful creature close to him, something he could never have hoped for in his wildest dreams.

Only once had he ever experienced anything nearly so exciting as this, during his second year at Heidelberg. With two or three of his fellow students he had gone out on the town celebrating a friend's birthday. They had spent a night of revelry in one of the less reputable beer gardens, and were ready for returning to their hostel when they saw three girls sitting at a corner table, and accepted an invitation to join them. One in particular had caught Rolf's eye. She was a dazzling beauty with raven hair which cascaded in ringlets down her back. He had been completely bewitched, and was flattered when she allowed him to see her to her lodgings on the outskirts of the town. Her name, he learned, was Margot. She was a shop assistant and had a room in the house of an elderly widower. When they reached the house she invited him to her room, and in a very short space of time the passionate kisses they shared led them to a more intimate relationship. His initial awkwardness was soon overcome by the experienced Margot, who knew all the weaknesses of men.

Rolf had asked to see Margot again the following weekend, and arranged a rendezvous at the same beer garden. He was there at the appointed time, and waited an hour without a sign of the girl. He was thinking of leaving when she arrived on the arm of another man, a rough looking character. They took a table quite near to Rolf and were soon head to head in a giggling conversation. From time to time they looked over to the table where Rolf sat alone, and laughed raucously.

She looked very different from the image Rolf had carried in his mind, and he began to have feelings of disgust. The memory of the incident had stayed with him, and whenever he thought of it he had a sensation of revulsion at his one night of foolishness. He acknowledged that the fault had been entirely his own, but it had served in later years as a suppression for his baser instincts.

There was no denying he wanted Daphne with a burning desire, but this was no sordid affair. He was going to make her his bride, but until they were man and wife, he would respect her virginity and refrain from causing her the kind of remorse he himself had experienced long ago.

Daphne had a strange sensation of wanting to be

possessed. The urge within her was driving her almost to distraction, and she responded to Rolf's kisses with an ecstatic eagerness. She could not trust herself, but she trusted Rolf, and knew that his love for her was strong enough to guide him to do what was right. Nothing would be lost to him by waiting until she was completely his.

When Rolf finally and reluctantly tore himself away, Daphne made her way to her room, got into bed and allowed herself the luxury of fantasy which led her into a sleep, bringing with it the kind of dreams which only the truly innocent can enjoy.

28

When Rolf reported to The Limes on Friday morning, the place was a hive of activity; people coming and going, women with cakes and men with garden produce, delivery vans and, most prominent of all, a lorry laden with marquees and tents. The rector was sitting at a trestle table endeavouring to deal with a constant string of queries. Where does this go? What shall I do with that? Who can I have to help me on this? What would you like me to do next?

Rolf was spared from having to wait in line for the rector's attention. Chris, who was engaged in conversation with the man delivering the marquees, saw Rolf from a distance and hailed him to come over to him.

'Mr Truscott wants us to supervise the erection of the marquees,' Chris told Rolf. 'We shall need all the able-bodied men we can muster. I've had a word with Father and he's sending two of the stable hands. Kitty's father may be coming shortly to lend a hand and the driver here will be staying until the job's done.'

Chris handed Rolf a copy of the plan which had been prepared, showing the proposed layout of the féte. There was an arena to be roped off where the fancy dress parade would assemble after it had paraded around the village. At the edge of the arena, a stand had already been erected for the use of the judges and any other officials, and it was here that the opening ceremony was to be performed.

Stan Croft and Alf Williams had been early on the scene to erect the refreshment tent, and their respective wives were busily engaged in handing out cups of tea and coffee to the workers. The driver left Chris and Rolf, and went over to avail himself of this facility. By the time he

184

returned, Chris had managed to raise a sufficiently large workforce to carry out the erection of the marquees. When this work had been completed there was a temporary fence to be erected around the perimeter of the lake. Notices already placed in the vicinity of this tempting stretch of water warned all those able to read that it was out of bounds.

Lots of side-shows were being erected all over the place and bunting in profusion was being hung. A huge banner across the entrance to The Limes proclaimed that a fête was to be held on this site. The success of earlier fétes had been such that the parochial church council felt justified in anticipating an attendance of at least two thousand people during the course of the day.

Charles Broxon approached Chris with an invitation for Rolf and himself to join a party of other workers for lunch at The Chequers. He gratefully accepted on behalf of them both, and when they arrived at the inn they found that the other workers invited were Daphne and Kitty, Mr and Mrs Glover and Mr and Mrs Charnford. Pat and Charles greeted them at the door and escorted them into their own private dining-room. The other guests were already assembled there and were enjoying pre-lunch drinks. There was a pleasant lack of formality; it was to be a buffet luncheon which the Broxons had prepared with infinite skill. Ted and Nancy were looking after the bar, but managed in between times to attend to the needs of the special guests.

Places had been set for eleven people although, including Charles and Pat, only ten were there. Before they took their places at the table, Charles called for silence; the door opened, and in walked a smart looking young soldier resplendent in uniform, with a broad grin on his face.

'Private Pattaway reporting for duty,' he said as he marched over to where Chris and Rolf were standing. They both showed their delight at seeing him and shook him warmly by the hand. He was introduced to the other guests and given a place of honour between Chris and Rolf.

'I'm goin' back ter take mi punishment, but I wanted ter

see yer first,' he told Chris.

'Now we must see what we can do to help,' Chris said.

'No, guvnor, I don't want no 'elp; I'm goin' ter take mi medicine,' the young man said with dignity. He explained that he had gone home to his parents and that his father, who had himself been a soldier, had told him what a fool he was to have got himself into trouble, and in no uncertain terms had insisted on the present course of action. The ladies were captivated by his Cockney charm; Mrs Charnford in particular would have willingly taken him under her maternal wing. Her husband, had circumstances been different, would have found him a job. However, as far as Alan was concerned, if the army wanted him, they were going to have him, whatever the consequences.

After lunch, Chris persuaded Alan to go along with the rest of them to The Limes. There was little work left to be done, and Colonel Briggs invited them all into the house. He was introduced to the young serviceman, who was clearly uncomfortable in such exalted company. However, the colonel quickly put him at his ease. Giving no sign of wanting to interfere, the older man talked in a friendly manner and Alan, without realising it, gave him all the information he might need to intercede with the military authorities.

It was with a certain amount of sadness that they wished Alan goodbye. They told him he would be welcome in Maresfield at any time, but Alan in his own way took a final leave of them. knowing that this was the end of a chapter in his life. He would always be a Londoner, but he would never forget these strange country people who seemed to live in a world of their own.

Before the gathering broke up, the Glovers reminded Rolf that he, along with Chris and Daphne, was to be their guest for dinner that evening.

'We shall expect you around eight o'clock. We've asked one or two other people along.'

There were four additional guests; the rector and Mrs Truscott, and Gordon and Myrtle Appleby. The Applebys, having spent most of their married lives in Sri Lanka where they managed a tea plantation, had always enjoyed an active social life in the colonial style. Their return to England had been a big disappointment to them, and they had not felt at ease in the kind of society The Park provided.

It was soon apparent that they were uncomfortable in the company of the Truscotts, and Gordon Appleby lost no time in letting it be known that he was in no way interested in the church or its garden fête. Connie Glover soon realised that it had been a mistake to invite them at the same time as the rector and his wife, but there was nothing she could do about it now, and the party was too small to keep them apart.

Conversation at the dinner table was kept at low key and the meal was a huge success. Connie had a reputation for her catering and this evening she had excelled herself. By tacit agreement, no mention was made of the fête, but Gordon Appleby persistently made skirmishes in the direction of the rector, and when the names of Peter Frobisher and Sir Harold Grantwell cropped up, he remarked, 'Doesn't say much for your Christianity, old chap, when two of your flock turn out to be high-powered criminals.'

The rector countered, 'But Mr Appleby, I can't think why their behaviour should have any bearing on my Christianity, as you put it. So far as I can remember, I have no recollection of either of the gentlemen in question having claimed to be Christians. You see, people come to church for many different reasons and, I must admit, often for the wrong reasons. If everyone who attended church was a saint, there would be no need for churches.'

Although Raymond Glover was unhappy at the turn which the conversation was taking, he could not resist the observation, 'You must agree, Gordon, they were rather astute in their choice of cover, and even if the rector had known they were villains he could hardly have had them blackballed.'

The rector continued, 'Perhaps Mr Appleby, I may one day have the pleasure of relieving you of the misapprehensions you appear to harbour concerning the Christian faith. I can't resist a challenge, but I'm sure you will agree that it would be inappropriate for us to cross swords now, in such congenial company.'

Appleby was forced by a sharp glance from his wife to bite his tongue. He would lose no time in getting even with this bumptious cleric, but here the odds were against him. He would seek satisfaction at the earliest opportunity. He was perfectly happy in his agnosticism, and was annoyed that this little incident was making him feel uncomfortable. What if he were wrong? Somehow, he was beginning to lose confidence in himself. Just supposing that after all there was something, someone somewhere, superior to Gordon Appleby? It didn't bear thinking about, but it wouldn't leave him. He was relieved when Myrtle reminded him that there were things to be done in readiness for their weekend away from the fairground atmosphere of Maresfield Park. The Truscotts declared themselves in need of an early night, and so the party broke up shortly after ten o'clock.

After they had gone, Connie heaved a visible sigh of relief and she apologised to her remaining guests for her lack of wisdom in her choice of guests.

'I shouldn't worry too much about it, my dear,' her husband consoled her. 'I was impressed by the way old Truscott handled Appleby. He's gone up a mile in my estimation.'

Mrs Glover was not so easily mollified. 'What must Rolf think of us?'

'I found it most interesting,' Rolf said. 'It has only served to enhance my opinion of the Reverend Mr Truscott, and what he said has set me thinking as to where I stand.'

'And me too!' said Chris. 'The few words he said have probably been more significant than a whole lot of his sermons.'

As Rolf walked Daphne home, very few words were spoken although there was much they both wanted to say. When they reached the door they stood in silence, their arms enfolding each other so tightly that it almost hurt. The first sound was a gentle sob from Daphne.

'My darling, what is it?' Rolf asked anxiously. 'I don't know. It's so silly, but I feel so very happy; I can't explain it. Oh Rolf I love you so very dearly.'

'Daphne, my dear, I find it difficult to explain the way I feel about you. All I can say is that having you by my side makes me so happy and my heart is overflowing.'

Their good night kiss was long and tender, interrupted at last by the sound of footsteps and a discreet cough which told them that Chris was returning home.

29

A light, early morning mist heralded a Saturday as glorious as any summer day on record. When Rolf rose from his bed the sun was already beginning to break through, and patches of blue sky gently insinuated themselves onto the canvas that was Maresfield on the morning of its summer fete. People were on the move in the village. Shopping had been finished early, all the cleaning work had been done, and anything not completed would have to be carried over until next week. Last minute adjustments were being made to fancy dress costumes. Children had been scrubbed, Maresfield was en fête and the air was charged with expectancy.

By nine o'clock, coming from all directions were figures in fancy dress, ranging from prosaic to original, from inspired to ingenious, all making their way towards the parade assembly point at Parklands. A coach carrying the Venturers' Carnival Band from Lewes had just arrived in the village. The driver brought it to a halt outside The Chequers and enquired the way to Parklands.

Punctually at a quarter to ten, the strains of a military march proclaimed to the world that the procession was setting out on its long circuitous route around the parish boundaries. There were tiny tots in fairylike costumes, nursery rhyme characters, spacemen, Wombles and decorated floats carrying throngs of happy children. Older people in the procession had gone to great lengths to enter into the spirit of the occasion. There were Cowboys and Indians on horseback, decorated bicycles, and one novel entrant was an attractive damsel dressed only in a large cardboard carton on which she announced her inability to take part in the contest, as she had nothing to wear.

The official party assembled in the large drawing-room at The Limes, where coffee was being served. A final briefing was given by the rector, and when the distant sound of drums and trumpets was heard, Rolf was escorted along with the other members of the ceremonial party, to the rostrum at the edge of the arena. Slowly the parade filed past the temporary dais and was martialled into position to await the judging. Admission to the fête was by programme and the first item on the programme, the opening ceremony, was about to commence.

Colonel Briggs had agreed to officiate as master of ceremonies, and after testing the microphone, began,

'Ladies and gentlemen, it is my very pleasant duty to introduce to you Herr Rolf Muller, a young man who came to this country only two weeks ago, but who has earned for himself a very special place in the hearts of all (or should I say, nearly all) those with whom he has come into contact. Now I am not here to make a speech and I know you'll be wanting to get down to the serious business of enjoying yourselves.' He turned to Rolf, indicating that he should be on his feet and ready to take over.

'Ladies and gentlemen, Herr Muller.'

Rolf was staggered by the enthusiastic reception he was given. It was at least five minutes before he was able to speak.

'Ladies and gentlemen,' he began, 'I am conscious of the very great honour The Reverend Mr Truscott has bestowed on me by inviting me to perform this opening ceremony. No doubt many of you will wonder, and even more so I myself wonder, why me? I do not have the answer and I will not bore you with theory, for I know you are all here to enjoy yourselves. I should like, however, to spend a few moments to offer my congratulations to all the people who have worked so very hard to organise this splendid occasion, not the least of whom is your worthy rector, The Reverend Percival Truscott. On behalf of Mr Truscott, I offer a special vote of thanks to our hosts, Colonel and Mrs Briggs, for their great kindness in providing this wonderful setting, and allowing us all to make use of their grounds. And now, without taking up any more of your time, I wish you all a most happy and memorable day, and ask you to give your whole-hearted support to the various events and sideshows. It gives me great pleasure to declare this fete open.'

The applause was generous, and it was some time before Colonel Briggs was able to announce that the judging of the fancy dress entries was about to commence. The recognised experts in the adjudication of carnival costume had been brought in from Brighton, and Rolf was more than happy to listen to what they had to say, and made only token comment on the things which struck him as being of particular interest.

He saw nothing of Daphne until it was time for lunch. She, along with Kitty, had been assisting Mrs Briggs in the preparation of a buffet luncheon provided for the official party. It was something of a disappointment to Rolf that Daphne was not able to sit alongside him, but she was kept busy, and he was in any case occupied most of the time with people he had not previously met and who wished to make his acquaintance. Eventually, Daphne took the opportunity to come over to where he was sitting, and they were able to make an arrangement to meet around two o'clock.

In the meantime, Chris found him and managed to drag him over to the coconut shy. This was something new in Rolf's experience, and he was content to stand and watch his friend collect coconuts, far too many to carry. The many children standing around gazed in admiration as the nuts continued to fall, and were rewarded with a share of the spoils. Rolf was able to show his prowess on the archery range, and by the time they were joined by Daphne and Kitty there were several trinkets for both girls. They walked from one stand to another giving support to the stallholders until the whole area of the fête had been covered.

It was a wonderful day; the grounds were thronged with people old and young carrying balloons, goldfish, coconuts and all the usual souvenirs of carnival time. Rolf declared he had never seen so many happy faces.

When they felt there was nothing more they could do to help things along at the fête, Rolf and Daphne decided to slip away for a while. They made their way down through the village to the Bells' cottage. When Grace heard Daphne announce herself, she called out for her to come in, and when she saw that Rolf was also there she exclaimed, 'Oh, and you too, Mr Muller. How very kind of you to come and see me when you must be so busy. Did you see Martin at the féte?'

'Yes, but only briefly,' Rolf replied. 'He was talking to the rector, and I just managed to say hello.'

'All my packing is done, and I'm ready for the great day,' Grace told them.

'My word, Mrs Bell, you're certainly well ahead of time. I've done none of mine yet, but we don't go until next Friday,' Daphne said.

'Yes, I keep telling Martin he can't wait to get me out of the way,' she responded with a chuckle, and then more seriously, 'If nothing else is achieved, it will give him a well-earned rest.'

Leaving Mrs Bell, they took a walk down a narrow tree-lined lane over to old Kitty Prewett's cottage. The door was ajar, and Daphne called out, 'It's Daphne and Mr Muller, may we come in?'

The old lady rose from her chair and walked over to the door to greet them. 'Well now, isn't this a lovely surprise? Come along and find a seat.'

They spent an hour with Mrs Prewett. She was thrilled to know that they had taken the trouble to come and see her when the rest of the village was occupied elsewhere. Rolf assured her that it would not be long before he came to England again, and promised that he would be sure to come and visit her.

30

The Sunday morning congregation at St Bartholomew's
was much larger than usual. Chris and Kitty, as well as
Kitty's parents, were there. Mrs Charnford was staying at
home this morning, but Daphne had arranged to go
along with Rolf, and he was to have lunch with the family.
They met at the entrance to the church car park, and
were astonished to see the number of cars parked there.

When they walked through the church doorway,
Martin Bell apologised that he couldn't find a place for
them near to where their friends were sitting. They were
obliged to move down to the front of the church, where
Prudence and Verity Smythe were able to make room for
them.

Albert Stanford was bringing his organ voluntary to a
close but, glancing up from the keys, he caught sight of
Rolf Muller and the young lady and extended his recital
by a good five minutes. The rector for once didn't seem to
mind being kept waiting. Organists of Mr Stanford's
calibre were a rare breed, and it was as well to remain on
good terms with the old gentleman. As Albert had so
often reminded him, music was as much a part of worship
as was the sermon.

The Reverend Percival was in tremendous form. It did
him a power of good to see all the pews occupied, and the
sight of so many new faces in the congregation inspired
him to discard the sermon he had prepared. For a long
time he remained quiet, as if waiting for divine guidance,
and then he said, 'Who is my neighbour?' A long pause
and then, 'When our Lord was asked this question, he
replied with a parable, the parable of The Good
Samaritan.'

'My neighbour is not necessarily the person who lives in

the next house. My neighbour is one who comes to me in times of trouble as well as in times of rejoicing. We people here in Maresfield might well take note of this analogy. Yesterday we were blessed with a day of rejoicing. Where we came from, it made no difference, we were united in one common cause. We should strive to maintain this spirit of neighbourliness which prevailed.'

There was no doubt that the rector's homily had served to make the people think, but Rolf and Daphne had their mind on other matters as they walked quietly towards home and lunch. Their meal was ready for them when they arrived. Mrs Charnford had made the most of her time at home and had left nothing for Daphne to do but entertain Rolf.

After they had lunched, Daphne insisted on taking over the task of clearing away the dishes and seeing to all the other chores which inevitably accumulate after a meal. The ladies agreed to share the work and while they were busy, Arthur Charnford invited Rolf to make an inspection of the farm with him. After a brief visit to the various farm buildings, they walked over the fields and Rolf was amazed at the vast acreage of land. He expressed his admiration for the wonderful condition of the crops. It was difficult for him to grasp how the comparatively few people he had seen working there were able to cultivate such a great expanse.

The fields of corn were ripe and golden, and Arthur Charnford expressed his gratitude for the fact that the fine weather looked like holding out for them to get the harvest in. 'We start in earnest tomorrow morning,' he said. 'Chris will be up early to get the men organised. It's going to be a case of all hands to the wheel.'
Rolf enjoyed the remainder of his walk, but remained fairly silent. He was turning something over in his mind.

They returned to the house to find the ladies waiting to give them coffee. They spent a pleasant afternoon just talking and, in general getting to know each other.

As Daphne and Rolf walked together in the garden, the young man said, 'Do you suppose I could make myself useful to your father in the harvest? I don't wish to get in the way, but I'd very much like to lend a hand, if he'll have me.'

'Rolf, are you quite sure? Daddy will be glad of all the help he can get, but it's hard work, you know.'

Mr Charnford was delighted with the offer of help and later on, when he and his wife were alone together, he remarked, 'You know, Sylvia, my love, the Lord has wonderfully blessed us with a wonderful son and a wonderful daughter, and now it looks as though he's going to bless us again with a wonderful son-in-law.'

Later in the evening, Chris brought Kitty home with him and a warm family atmosphere was created. They had a very light meal together and afterwards they gathered round the piano and sang songs. Some Rolf knew and some he didn't, but it made no difference. It reminded him so much of home, and the added pleasure of listening to the voice of his Daphne made it all perfect.

Chris was glad of the extra help they were to have with the harvest, and felt a warm glow at the thought of once again labouring side by side with his friend Rolf.

'We shall be starting at the crack of dawn,' Chris said. 'You'll have to ask Pat Broxon to give you a six o'clock breakfast.' There was a mischevous glint in his eye as he said this.

'He'll do no such thing,' Daphne cried out. 'Breakfast here will be at six thirty, won't it Mummy?'

Her mother agreed that that would indeed be the time, and she said Rolf must come and have breakfast with them.

It was a strenuous day in the harvest field, particularly so for Rolf. However, he was rewarded by the sight of Daphne coming across the fields with a basket containing tea and scones for morning elevenses. She also encouraged him by telling him he was to have lunch with the family. Chris strolled over to them and expressed his gratitude for the assistance given and said that if the work proceeded at the rate already achieved, they would be completely finished harvest by Wednesday evening.

By the time Rolf returned to The Chequers in the early evening he was tired but contented. He had done, for the first time in his life, a hard manual task, but it was an achievement which was highly satisfying.

The same pattern was repeated on the next day, and the day after that. Life on the farm was at its busiest peak. There was little time for leisure and apart from meal times, Rolf saw little of Daphne. The few brief interludes they had together were sweet and served to enhance their longing for each other's company. They were both glad when the evening came and the work finally done.

It was after ten o'clock on Thursday morning before Rolf woke up. It was a knock at his door which roused him, and Charles Broxon came into his room with a cup of coffee. The inkeeper was in a jovial mood and stayed on a little with his guest. 'I trust you slept well,' he said. 'You'll need to be astir before this time tomorrow morning or you'll miss the ferry.'

As he put out his hand to take the cup of coffee, Charles noticed the blisters which were beginning to form. 'Rolf, you'll have to see a doctor,' he quipped. 'You'll never drive across Europe with those hands.'

Rolf had no reply to Charles' banter. Instead he said, 'I shall be glad when tomorrow morning comes; I don't mean by that that I shall be glad to leave Maresfield. On the contrary, it's been wonderful here. I shall always remember the kindness you have shown me, Charles. Maybe some day you will come to Germany and give me the opportunity of reciprocating what you have done.'

'Rolf, it's been a pleasure having you as a guest here. Apart from the actual pleasure of having you with us, you have worked wonders for my trade. Don't forget, we are expecting you here for Ted's wedding. I'm afraid we shan't be able to accommodate you then. We'll be more than full on that occasion, but I've no doubt there are lots of homes in Maresfield where you'll be welcome. You've made a tremendous impression on this village. I'm sure it can never be the same again.'

The day passed peacefully, giving Rolf time to relax in readiness for a long return journey home. He made several calls to say goodbye to his new friends, and had a quiet evening at the Charnford home.

31

The staff at The Lintzen Clinic were unusually excited as they awaited the arrival of the young Herr Doktor Rolf, son of the professor, Herr Direktor Muller. Fraulein Beckmann, the matron, had briefed them concerning the special English patient who was being brought this morning, together with an English nurse.

Fraulein Beckmann was a kindly soul; she had reached the age of retirement and was, in fact, due to leave this very week, but the Herr Direktor had specially requested that she should stay on for a while, partly because of her exceptional nursing skill, but chiefly because of her ability to converse fluently in English. One or two of the junior nurses had a knowledge of English and were looking forward to the opportunity of putting it into practice.

When the small party arrived at the clinic, Rolf's father was there to meet them. There was no mistaking who he was. Daphne was amazed at the striking resemblance between father and son. He greeted his son with a warm affection. Rolf introduced Mrs Bell to him and she was immediately assured of the warmth and reality of the welcome.

The older man turned to the younger lady accompanying them and Rolf hastened to make the further introduction. 'Father, I'd like you to meet Miss Charnford. Daphne, as you will have gathered, this is my father.'

'How do you do, Miss Charnford? Welcome to The Lintzen Clinic. I understand we are to have the pleasure of your company at our home. Now let me introduce you to our dear Fraulein Beckmann, who is our matron and a very good friend of my family. Fraulein Beckmann, will you show Miss Charnford the clinic and have Mrs Bell made comfortable while my son and I have a talk?'

Rolf accompanied his father to his private quarters, a comfortable, well appointed suite of offices which, in time of emergency, afforded a place to sleep and have meals. Coffee was brought in and the two men sat down to have their talk.

'Father, I want to tell you that Daphne is rather more than just a travelling companion for Mrs Bell. You will possibly think I am acting irresponsibly, but I am deeply in love with her.'

Rolf waited for the announcement to sink in, expecting some form of minor explosion. When his father spoke, it was in a soft, gentle tone. 'My son, the young lady is undoubtedly very beautiful and I can understand how you feel about her. However, after such a short acquaintance, was it wise to bring her all the way from England to stay with us?'

'Father,' said Rolf, 'she has come in the first place to accompany Mrs Bell who would not have been able to make the journey without the assistance of another woman, and you yourself made this stipulation. It was not Daphne's wish that she should stay anywhere but at the clinic, and she volunteered to work here without payment in order to ease the burden on your staff. Her family have been most generous to me in their hospitality, and I owe it to them to see that she is made welcome in our country.'

'Rolf, we will do all we can to help you make her stay in Germany a memorable and a happy one,' his father said. 'I'm sure you are sensible enough to know what you are doing. You are my son and I trust your judgement. Take her as soon as you can to your mother and Helga. They are impatient to meet her, and they won't be disappointed.'

Frau Muller had been warned by telephone that her son and the young English lady were on their way. As soon as they saw Rolf's blue Mercedes turn into the drive, mother and daughter hurried to the door to greet them. Frau Muller was very much like Daphne's own mother. She didn't wait for an introduction, but stretched out her hand and clasped her young guest warmly, saying, 'I am very happy to welcome you to our home.'

Helga in the meantime was busy hugging her elder brother, and it took some little time for him to be able to greet his mother.

'You must be Helga,' Daphne said, 'Rolf has told me so much about you.'

Helga took her hand and led her indoors saying, 'Come, let me take you to your room.'

It was a beautiful room with a view overlooking a garden ablaze with flowers of all kinds, stretching all the way down to the river. As Daphne unpacked her luggage, Helga lay on the bed admiring the pretty clothes that were being transferred from case to wardrobe. She could not take her eyes off Daphne and several times, to Daphne's embarrassment murmured, 'You are so beautiful.' This coming from a young woman as attractive as Helga undoubtedly was, was complimentary indeed, and there was no doubting the girl's sincerity.

Rolf's father arrived home in the early evening, and they sat down to dinner. He told them that Mrs Bell was settling quite satisfactorily and had already endeared herself to the nurses at the clinic. It would be difficult, he said, to assess the length of time she would be required to stay at The Lintzen, but he thought it would be at least six weeks. The first stages of the treatment would involve the gradual reduction in the quantity of drugs she was taking, until eventually she would be off them completely. There would then be a brief period of experimentation with a new, externally applied substance which had recently been developed, but was not yet universally available.

They spent a very pleasant evening together, Daphne showing photographs of her family which she had brought along with her, and telling the Mullers all about her life in Maresfield. Rolf had to endure the embarrassment of his mother showing snapshots of himself as a baby and when he could endure it no longer, he suggested an evening stroll along the river bank. Daphne had thought that meant herself and Rolf, but no, the whole family came along. Her surprise abated somewhat when she perceived that it was customary amongst the Germans to take their evening walk in a family unit. She rather liked the idea, and thought how much better it would be if English families returned to this way of life.

Daphne visited the clinic regularly, along with Rolf. She was always made to feel welcome, but Fraulein Beckmann would not hear of her doing any form of work. It was a delight for her to see Mrs Bell each day looking so much better, and the old lady was happy to see how things were between Rolf and Daphne. She sent cheerful letters home to Martin, giving him every reason to hope for a tremendous improvement in her condition.

Daphne made several half-hearted references to the fact that she ought to be getting back home, but the Mullers would not listen. They had taken her very much to their hearts. She was having a wonderful time in Germany, although her proposed visit to her friend in Iserlohn seemed to have been forgotten.

Daily, her love for Rolf was growing stronger and stronger, and he had no difficulty in convincing his family that there could never be any other girl in his life. There was no doubt in their minds either, and already they were treating her as a member of their family.

It was a letter from home that finally made up her mind that she should go back to England. Mr and Mrs Glover had arranged a party for Kitty and Chris, at which they were to announce their engagement to be married.

'Rolf, darling, I can't miss this. Will you take me?' Daphne asked.

'Do you think I could possibly stay away?' he said. 'But wouldn't it be better to make it a double celebration?'

'What do you mean, Rolf?' she asked.

He stood for a moment looking into her eyes, and after he had kissed her long and passionately he said, 'Daphne, darling, will you marry me?'

'Oh, Rolf, please say it again,' she murmured.

'Will you marry me, darling?' he asked.

'Oh yes, Rolf, I will!' she said.